To David Kirkpatrick,
"my favorite mogul"

Humanely yours,

Gary Kalur

MONSTERS AND MIRACLES

Henry Bergh's America

a biographical novel
by
Gary Kaskel

Copyright © 2013 by Gary Kaskel

Edited by Arthur Gordon

Cover design by Dennis Woloch
Henry Bergh painting by John Wood Dodge courtesy the ASPCA
Author photo by Susan Weingartner
"The Crowded Car" illustration by Sol Eytinge, Jr.
Mary Ellen Wilson photo courtesy of the George Sim Johnston Archives of The
    New York Society for the Prevention of Cruelty to Children

ISBN 978-0-7414-9804-5 Paperback
ISBN 978-0-7414-9805-2 eBook
Library of Congress Control Number: 2013914404

Printed in the United States of America

Published October 2013

INFINITY PUBLISHING
1094 New DeHaven Street, Suite 100
West Conshohocken, PA 19428-2713
Toll-free (877) BUY BOOK
Local Phone (610) 941-9999
Fax (610) 941-9959
Info@buybooksontheweb.com
www.buybooksontheweb.com

*Dedicated to the men and women
who had—and continue to have—the courage
to follow in Henry Bergh's footsteps.*

TABLE OF CONTENTS

Prologue 1

Chapter 1 13

Chapter 2 19

Chapter 3 31

Chapter 4 41

Chapter 5 49

Chapter 6 63

Chapter 7 79

Chapter 8 93

Chapter 9 113

Chapter 10 131

Chapter 11 149

Chapter 12 167

Chapter 13 181

Chapter 14 191

Chapter 15 203

Chapter 16 217

Epilogue 225

Author's Notes 229

Illustrations 231

PROLOGUE

What drives humans to endeavors of great challenges can often be traced to conscious or unconscious introspection of our personal issues: self-esteem, social status, peer pressure, creativity, sexuality, faith, greed, altruism, paternal/maternal instincts, indignation, outrage, denial of mortality and the list continues.

Both large and small movements in matters of social justice do not come easily. The men and women who challenge the status quo often suffer professionally and personally. They endure criticism, derision and sometimes physical jeopardy because they believe if they do not take up the cause, no one else will. That sense of duty comes at various stages in life. Some are virtually born with it and become active early in life. Others discover it later as the process of living educates and informs the previously ignorant. Change arrives when one realizes that the time has come to act and take personal responsibility. This can happen slowly or as a watershed moment, but when it happens, the person making the change will never be the same again.

Henry Bergh was born on August 29, 1813, in New York City, the youngest of three children born to Christian Bergh III of Rhinebeck-on-the-Hudson, New York, and Elizabeth Ivers of Connecticut. The Swedish-born Christian Bergh designed and built ships. He had moved to New York shortly after the American Revolution to raise his family in a small house on the corner of Scammel and Water Streets, across from the shipyards along the East River in lower Manhattan.

By the War of 1812, Christian Bergh had built a thriving business with a reputation for honesty and high quality and supplied the U.S. Navy with frigates to

fight the British. The Bergh children, Edwin, Jane and
Henry, grew up around the shipyard. Their father had a
reputation as a perfectionist and man of integrity,
becoming known in the neighborhood as "the honestest
man in New York." He was an imposing figure of six feet
two inches and had a commanding presence over the
hundreds of carpenters and workmen he supervised. He
was also a proud Andrew Jackson Democrat with an
independent spirit in the pre-Abolition days by being
the first New York shipbuilder to employ workers of
color.

Young Henry Bergh thus grew up in affluence with a
strong role model. His father had both business acumen
and political influence, conferring with leaders from
Tammany Hall and chairing political meetings. His
social circle included successful businessmen, politicians
and other influential New Yorkers. During Henry's teen
years, Jacob A. Westervelt was a fixture around the
Bergh household. He began as Dad's apprentice and
showed enough skill and promise to start his own
shipbuilding business in Charleston, South Carolina. In
1822, Westervelt moved back to New York, became a
business partner of Dad's and would later become an
alderman and then the mayor of New York.

Henry's mother, Elizabeth, was also a strong
influence, home-schooling him and instilling within her
son the virtues of honesty and duty that her husband
exemplified. She recognized that her youngest child was
a sensitive boy, quite the opposite of his older brother,
Edwin. When Henry was eleven years old, he and
another boy were playing by the docks at the shipyard
when Henry lost his footing and fell into the East River.
Henry almost drowned before getting rescued, as he
later put it, "by a meddlesome person [who] pulled me
out and saved me to become a plague and nuisance in
New York City and to endure miserable colds." It
appeared that the youth was not interested in a nautical

life or livelihood and took more interest in literature and the arts. Young Henry was an avid reader and practiced his penmanship diligently.

As he grew, Henry paid meticulous attention to his wardrobe and grooming and had an unmistakable eye for the ladies for whom he began writing poetry. By age seventeen he reached the height of his father and began sporting a mustache. With his soulful blue eyes and thick mop of brown hair, he became a popular and randy young bachelor, having the good looks and financial means to entertain young ladies. He worked in his father's office by day, but left the drudgery of common office work as soon as possible to attend theatrical shows in the Bowery and dine with his friends and latest lady love. His mother worried that her younger son would become a dilettante, and it appeared she might be right. While his older brother Edwin had graduated with honors from Georgetown University, Henry started attending Columbia College on nearby Church Street, but didn't stay long enough to graduate with his class of 1834. He preferred getting dressed in his finest clothes and going out dining, dancing and leading the life of a young aristocrat.

Sex in those days could be an elusive and frustrating goal for a bachelor, even a well-heeled one. Henry lost his virginity, as many boys did, with the help of his older pal, Henry Brevoort, who arranged a liaison with a fabulous prostitute who was not only well-endowed but also well-read. Brevoort was a man of the world and wealthy landowner who lived in a mansion on the Bowery with a private menagerie comprising at various times exotic birds, deer, a bear and two tigers that he kept chained in his watermelon patch. He was also a man of great literary taste whose lifelong friendship with Washington Irving, author of *Sleepy Hollow* and *Rip Van Winkle*, was one he cherished. He also had a proclivity for wild times with multiple sex partners and other fetishes and devoted a basement "cavern," as he called it, to such activities. Only the wealthy could afford to carry on in such luxury and not be discovered. Brevoort's friendship with young Henry Bergh afforded him opportunities to meet younger women. Before Brevoort married, he dismantled the downstairs room and put the furnishings in storage. His wife never learned of her husband's taste for the perverse, although he managed to get away for erotic trysts with various New York women, most of whom were prostitutes.

Henry Bergh's first sexual experience was life-changing, inasmuch as at age seventeen he was emotionally immature and fell madly in love with his hired partner, a tall raven-haired Irish beauty named Hannah. Her piercing blue eyes melted the boy's heart, and her uninhibited, carefree attitude toward sex was something he dared not express on his own outside of her boudoir. What would people think? He continued to procure her for months and had proposed marriage to her at the end of almost every visit, to which she laughed lightheartedly and graciously declined the boy's sweet offer. Less than a year went by when, suddenly, Hannah disappeared. She vacated her apartment, and the neighbors had no information as to where she had gone. Perplexed and heartbroken, Henry made several efforts to find her, but to no avail. For the rest of his life he had a taste and strong desire for the Black Irish, which was never satisfied the way it was with Hannah.

In his twenties, Henry Bergh was a young man without any direction beyond his hedonistic desires to have fun dining out at fashionable restaurants, attending the theater and drinking in the salons of his upper-class friends where discussions about politics, religion and the arts were stimulating but rarely transformative. Henry was a lad who had it made in this world, but whose quest for true happiness went beyond his material wealth and always came back to the same lovelorn desire for a mate.

New Year's was a holiday that young men and women always looked forward to, as it had become a custom on New Year's Day for the ladies to stay home and receive gentlemen callers with offerings of food and drink. The young men would dress in their finest clothes and go from door to door, visiting the various single ladies in the neighborhood and spending time as their guests, with both parties hoping to make a special connection. The young ladies looked forward to offering their feminine hospitality as much as the young men did and dressed in their finest petticoats and jewels to receive the suitors.

And so it was on New Year's Day of 1839 when Henry Bergh rang the bell at 90 Warren Street, home of a wealthy Englishman named Thomas Taylor, to call on his daughter, Catherine Matilda, whose dark hair and youthful good looks had attracted Henry's attention some months earlier during a visit to Conoit's Ice Cream Garden, where they both frequented in the summer. He was welcomed in and a couple was quickly formed.

Henry and Matilda became inseparable, and the good-looking pair were often seen dining out, dancing at parties, strolling down the promenade at Battery Park and riding in a hansom to the destination of their latest social event. Henry knew she was a virgin, and after failing to gently persuade her to give up her chastity— after all, you can't blame a fellow for trying—she let it be known that she was saving herself for marriage. So, Henry proposed, and a wedding was set for noon on September 10, 1839, at old St. Mark's, a prestigious center of religious and social events. The two prominent families planned for a large wedding, and announcements appeared in several of the newspapers, sparking a lot of talk among the wealthy social circles of lower Manhattan.

Upon the arrival of the wedding date, early on the morning of September the 10th, as many a groom before him, Henry was wracked with panic attacks. The twenty-six-year-old couldn't face the crowds anticipated to witness their wedding vows. He secretly escaped the house and traveled to the Taylors's house, where he managed to persuade Matilda to duck the crowd at the church and elope with him. Fearing he would back out of the marriage and pitying her fiancé's fragile mental state, Matilda went along and threw etiquette out the window. The two got married before the guests even arrived at St. Mark's. Although disappointed, the families still gave a wedding reception and champagne supper for their invitees, at which the newlyweds made a brief appearance to save face. Many parents are relieved that their offspring finally wed, and it's fair to say that Christian and Elizabeth Bergh were among them.

Henry and Matilda's early married life was filled with setting up house, social events, travel, fine dining and a nervous intimacy. Prior to marriage, Henry had already been with several women, but he knew his bride was a virgin, making their first time together an awkward one. Henry's sheer physical size was problematic for the diminutive Matilda, who experienced an unpleasant first time. After that, things got better, but there was always an apprehension from both sides when approaching moments of intimacy that was a psychological barrier to having fully satisfying relations. There were few experts in whom to confide such issues, and both were too modest to consult with friends, and so a silent tolerance grew between them that was a resignation of what their lives together was going to be like. Their genuine love and respect for one another was stronger than any other aspect of their relationship. And for all outward appearances, they remained a perfect couple.

Four years after Henry and Matilda's wedding, Christian Bergh died, followed by Henry's mother three years after that. Henry sold his interest in the family business, Bergh & Co., to his father's partner, Jacob Westervelt. He also sold his share of the considerable land his parents had owned, providing him a considerable fortune. By that time, many of the old aristocracy in lower Manhattan had begun moving uptown to brownstone townhouses on Fifth Avenue, and Henry and Matilda joined them by moving to the corner of Twenty-second Street.

But the world was changing in old New York, as these were days of social unrest, culminating with the bread riots, abolition riots, anti-German demonstrations and bloody hand-to-hand combat among Irish laborers on the new Croton aqueduct, which changed the peaceful New York of Henry Bergh's youth.

It was time to get away from such conflict and ugliness, and the Berghs had the resources and desire to travel, since they had no obligations keeping them at home. For wealthy heirs who led aimless lives, travel became a way to fill the days. For the next decade, the Berghs spent fewer than half their days in New York, bouncing back and forth between Europe, Saratoga in Upstate New York and Washington, D.C., where Henry's friendship with President Lincoln's future Secretary of State, William Seward, would later pay off with a diplomatic appointment. But Europe was having its own riots in the troubled 1840s and 1850s. Fortunately, Henry had friends in diplomatic circles who managed to advise him where to go and where to avoid. And so the Berghs traveled throughout Europe in style. Unfortunately, all the traveling began to take its toll on Matilda, who began suffering from various illnesses from headaches and colds to lethargy and poor digestion. Henry would often attend events and visit sites without her, making sure that she was attended by the best local doctors back at their hotels.

Henry Bergh was infinitely curious about the peoples of other cultures, and he made it a point to seek out and dine at the local restaurants where the working class ate. He would bring his journal wherever he went and write notations about his experiences. Bergh's efforts as an author were sincere, but met with less than enthusiasm. His poems were published in various volumes and papers with rarely anyone taking notice. He began writing plays with titles, such as *The Streets of New York*, *Love's Alternative*, *The Portentious Telegram* and *The Ocean Paragon*, many of which dwelled on male-female relationship issues, no doubt reflecting Henry's own conflicted feelings on love and passion and the opposite sex. The critics either ignored or skewered them when Henry managed to get a theater company to perform them. And while these efforts went unrewarded, Henry continued to express himself with his creative writing, seeking the approval all artists seek. As the years passed, intimate relations with his wife became lukewarm, and writing became therapeutic for Henry, and often such inner turmoil would find its way onto the stage.

* * *

On a mild winter evening in 1862, a horse-drawn carriage pulls up to the Brooklyn Academy of Music, delivering an elderly couple dressed in formal wear who head for the main entrance. The man checks his pocket watch as he gets out and turns back to his wife, declaring, "We're thirty minutes late, for heaven's sake."

The woman apologizes, "I'm sorry, dear."

They rush past the glass-encased poster for tonight's performance that reads, "*Married Off*—a drama in verse by Henry Bergh."

Inside the theater, the well-dressed audience is listening to the actors on a stage that is illuminated with gaslight. The stage setting is the parlor of a well-appointed home. There are two actors onstage, a man and a woman playing the parts of Rose and Hannibal, a couple whose marriage is apparently in decline. Some of the audience members are listening intently, while others seem bored, as they listen to the dialogue.

"I fear we were fast to marry, for, tho' your ambition lay in shirt collars, by your father's last will, our marriage would fill your pockets with thousands of dollars," says Rose.

Hannibal responds, "Knowing my amiable weakness, in your parlor one night did you with brandy excite me and then make me promise to marry."

She counters forlornly, "The success, which we have recorded, was purely selfish and sordid for us both."

"Your reputation is not a sport, m'dear," he returns.

"If the belles of the day saw naught to admire, nor my gentle nature inspire, those icebergs of pride have but philanthropy's pride."

Up in a box sits Henry and Matilda Bergh, the play's author and his wife, now a middle-aged couple who are dressed in formal clothes. He sports long pork-chop sideburns, and she is holding his hand as he listens attentively to the actors on stage and occasionally appears to repeat their dialogue to himself. Periodically he scans the audience, watching for reactions.

"So, your motto is caveat emptor?" Hannibal asks.

"Marriage, my dearest Hannibal, to some is a manacle. To others, merely a spectacle. But this one, however unpleasant the speech, we are free to admit, partook much of each," Rose tells him.

"Malice among friends—detraction and slander—are like sauces to fish, or to any good dish. For a sauce to the goose is a sauce to the gander."

She responds to the insult, "My dear mother always told me duplicity is useful complicity. For it is easy, be the truth spoken, to lead men of wit, blindfold into a pit. But not so easy with their eyes wide open."

As Henry observes the audience, he sees one older man asleep, another one yawning and a woman in the middle of the orchestra section whispering to her companion with a cupped hand.

"You have, my dear Rose, the incense of soul, the homage which beauty, faith and duty inspire a feeling beyond your control," Hannibal continues.

"Is your worldly assessment of our marital bliss, that wives will become passé and will not improve like good wine by their age?" she asks.

"I hold certain symptoms of humanity's doom, as the Rose is certainly losing its bloom."

The bitter-edged drama does not sit well with all the patrons. One audience member in the orchestra section below catches the author's eye as he gets up and gestures to his lady to follow. The two quietly walk up the aisle and exit the theater, dropping the program on the floor on their way out.

Henry tries to hide any emotion as the two exit early, as Matilda silently squeezes his hand sympathetically.

Illus. 1 - drawing of young Henry Bergh

Illus. 2 - photograph of young Henry Bergh

CHAPTER 1

It's a picture postcard day in Upstate New York in October of 1952. Orange and golden leaves dot the streets and lawns as a tan Chevy Bel-Air station wagon travels northbound on the rural route that will take its occupants to their destination, the home of Mrs. Mary Ellen Schutt. The Mills Brothers singing "The Glow Worm" is playing on the radio.

The vehicle is carrying a three-person crew from CBS Television in Manhattan. The driver is Allen Waggoner, a producer of morning newscasts for the past year until the network gave him the promotion to weekend programming. At least he sees it as a promotion, even though the salary isn't any better. Wearing the same brown suit he wore when he first interviewed for the job, Waggoner is all business, the kind that an old newspaper man is known for, as he listens to his notes being read aloud for the interview they are about to shoot.

Reading from a notepad is Joan Hammer, a young, auburn-haired associate producer whose pencil behind her ear belies her no-nonsense approach to research and the work ethic of a first-generation television journalist who aspires to be an on-camera reporter someday. Joan speaks loudly to compete with the Mills Brothers.

In the backseat is a jacketless Jed Talbert, a husky young man wearing a fedora and looking out the window. Jed is the camera operator. His father was a newsreel cameraman who trained him at the Paramount Studios in Long Island City as a teenager. Apprenticing was fine, but when a friend at CBS Television offered him a steady job working in the city where he could shoot sixteen millimeter film and wouldn't have to lug around the heavy thirty-five millimeter cameras the newsreels require, it was a no-brainer. And Dad couldn't be prouder, especially on the rare occasion when the two would cover the same event.

"Mrs. Schutt is eighty-eight years old and has total recall, according to her daughter," Joan says while flipping the pages in her notepad.

"Good. Being a witness to history is always better when you can remember things."

"Here it is." She stops on a page and reads. "The trial began in April of 1874 when she was nine years old."

"Do we have any transcripts?" Allen asks.

"Not yet. Because it was a juvenile case, the records are usually sealed. But because of the age of this case, my contact in the clerk's office thinks he can get the administrative judge to release them."

"Good."

Joan continues reading, "There were several witnesses called, but the condition of the child was what cinched the case."

"Let me ask you this," Allen interjects. "Do you think Mrs. Schutt has seen the photos taken at the time, and if not, she'll object to our showing them onscreen? Did you get any sense of her attitude today from your phone conversation?"

"Hard to tell. She seemed very sweet. Didn't appear to be harboring any animosity or resentment about the whole thing. Was interested in giving credit where credit was due."

"So this lady has been living in obscurity for almost eighty years, and you were the only one who was able to find her? Good work, kiddo."

Avoiding the compliment, Joan continues, "Do you want to hear the questions?"

"Sure."

The Mills Brothers are finishing up singing.

I got a gal that I love so
Glow little glow-worm, glow
Glow little glow-worm, glow
Glow little glow-worm, glow.

Allen reaches over and turns off the radio, as Joan reads from her pad.

It's just before eleven when the station wagon with a small decal of the famous CBS eye affixed to the rear window arrives at the modest home of Mrs. Schutt. The craftsman-style house is on a quiet street that is punctuated by the faint smell of burning leaves from a neighbor the next block over disposing of the fall's remnants.

The first one out of the car is Jed, who quickly moves to the rear and opens the tailgate where his equipment lies. He begins unloading lights, light stands, a wooden tripod and a wooden case containing the Auricon sixteen millimeter sound camera. Allen steps out and straightens his necktie in his reflection in the driver's window, then takes out a pocket comb and runs it through his straight brown hair earlier laced with half a palm full of Vitalis. Joan remains in the passenger seat arranging her notes, which she places in her shoulder bag and then begins looking for a lipstick.

Inside the house, Mrs. Schutt's daughter, Etta, a lanky sixty-five-year-old wearing a brown pin-striped pants suit, sees the vehicle in the driveway and calls out to her mother, "Mother, the television people are here." She walks to the sunroom, where white-haired Mary Ellen sits in her favorite chair by the window, dressed in a floral print gingham dress, looking reminiscent of a Norman Rockwell portrait.

"Did you make iced tea?" the elderly woman asks.

"Yes, Mother. And lemonade. And sandwiches for later."

"Good." Then the doorbell rings and Etta turns and leaves the room.

"Hello," Etta exclaims as she opens the front door. "I'm Etta, Mary Ellen's daughter." Allen greets her and introduces his colleagues. Etta explains where her mother is and suggests that the sunroom would be a nice place to film the interview, if they like it. Allen turns to Jed and thinks the light might be good there. Jed agrees, but wants to take a look first. Etta escorts the trio through the house to the rear where the sunroom is bathed with the midmorning sunshine that forms a halo like rim on the top of Mary Ellen's hair. The four enter the room, and the visitors introduce themselves politely to the aging matriarch, who remains seated due to nagging arthritis and the familiar comfort of her favorite reading chair.

They agree that the room is an excellent location to film, and Jed exits to retrieve his gear while Allen and Joan exchange pleasantries about the scenic area with Mrs. Schutt. Returning moments later loaded down with cases, Jed begins to set up his camera equipment and lights. Allen and Joan move chairs so they can sit next to the camera and face Mrs. Schutt.

"Your daughter tells us that you have an excellent memory, Mrs. Schutt," Allen says with a strong voice and leaning toward her.

"Yes. And my hearing is fine, too," she smiles.

Allen sheepishly returns the smile and leans back in the chair, picking up his clipboard. "Yes. Sorry. We'll get started in a few minutes, but I'd like to explain our interview style first before we begin. I will ask you the questions, but you will not hear my voice in the program, so I ask that you try to answer in full sentences and perhaps incorporate my question in your answer, if you can. This will be very easy, because it's all from your memory of the events. Plain and simple. Just tell us your story, Mrs. Schutt."

"Certainly. But, please call me Mary Ellen. That's my name."

"Of course. Thank you." Allen turns to Jed, "How're we doing?"

Jed is adjusting the photo floodlight so it shines on the subject. "About a minute."

"Great," his producer replies.

Etta enters the room holding a tray of glasses. "Who would like iced tea or lemonade? I made both." After distributing drinks, it's time to get started. Allen asks Jed to start filming, and a beat later Jed looks through the viewfinder and responds, "Rolling."

In front of the camera, Joan holds up a CBS-TV slate and clapboard that reads, "Program: Witness to History; Subject: Mary Ellen Schutt; Date: 10-4-52; Producer: Allen Waggoner." She speaks the program name along with Mary Ellen's name and then claps the clapper and sits back down. Although this is all new and exciting for Mrs. Schutt and her daughter, they remain as observant and composed as New Yorkers typically are.

Mrs. Schutt looks at the camera and then to Allen. "Do I look at you?"

"Yes, just ignore the camera. Speak to me." He smiles to reassure her and then speaks to her directly. "If I could begin, could you tell us when and where you were born and raised?"

Mary Ellen responds. "I was born in New York City, in Manhattan, in 1864, during the Civil War. My birth name was Mary Ellen Wilson. My father died soon after I was born, and my mother had to work and did not make enough money to support me, so I was given up to foster care with the McCormicks, Mary and Thomas. We lived in a tenement on West Forty-first Street.

"What do you recall about your foster mother, Mary McCormick?"

"She had no time to take care of me, so she treated me poorly."

Allen looks up from his notes, "She abused you pretty badly?"

"Yes. She beat me regularly. I never knew why," she recounts matter-of-factly.

"Any ideas?"

"My stepmother was a women who had lost a husband before I arrived, remarried a man who drank too much, lived in dire poverty. I guess she just had a difficult time dealing with her circumstances."

"How old were you at this time?"

"It started when I was around six. It was a terrible thing for a young girl to suffer like that. I owe my survival to two people: Etta Wheeler, who I named my first daughter after, and Henry Bergh. But it was really Mr. Bergh who made them listen."

"Tell us about Mr. Bergh."

Mary Ellen takes a deep breath and exhales. "They called him the Great Meddler, the newspapers did. He came from a wealthy family in New York. Made their fortune in shipbuilding, I believe. President Lincoln made Mr. Bergh an ambassador to St. Petersberg, Russia, during the war."

CHAPTER 2

Despite the frigid temperature in St. Petersberg Square, the human participants in the afternoon traffic of carriages, pushcarts and pedestrians all have one common goal: to get out of the cold. A fine carriage pulled by two horses makes its way through the light snow of the Russian winter of 1863.

Inside the carriage sits Henry Bergh, a dour-looking, fifty-something man sporting pork-chop sideburns, dressed in diplomatic attire replete with top hat, medals and a multicolored sash across his chest. Using a quill pen, he is writing in a folded parchment. Beside him is his wife, Matilda, whose matronly appearance masks an attractive, middle-aged woman who is devoted to her mate.

Ambassador Bergh dips the quill into an inkwell that is built into the outside armrest, then looks up from writing in his journal, "I am not looking forward to lunch with Count Stanislav. He eats like a Cossack and tells war stories at such length that I wish he'd never received a commission."

"Now, Henry, be nice. We are representing the U.S. of A. and the food at La Vielle Russe is quite excellent. Perhaps the count will bring his lovely niece. What was her name?"

"Violetta," Henry responds.

"You always remember the pretty ones, don't you?"

"I remember that she sings like a songbird. If she ever comes to America, I should bring her to John Selwyn to put her on the stage."

There is a commotion outside, consisting of horses whinnying, a man yelling and a whip cracking. Henry looks out the window to observe a peasant who is severely whipping a horse because the cart it is pulling

19

has one broken wheel and moves with great difficulty. Henry calls out to the driver to stop the carriage. He gets out and signals the carriage driver to get down and follow him as he approaches the peasant.

"Tell him to stop that," Henry directs the driver.

The driver calls out in Russian to the peasant. The diminutive peasant looks up, surprised by the interruption.

Henry continues, "Ask him why he is whipping that poor beast when it is his fault the cart is broken?"

The driver complies and again speaks to the peasant in Russian. The peasant turns and looks at the six-foot two-inch Henry Bergh dressed in the finest diplomatic attire and becomes frightened.

"Ваша светлость, если я не приеду домой до захода солнца мне и моей лошади и замерзнуть до смерти," the peasant says sheepishly.

The driver turns to his employer, "He addresses you as 'Your lordship,' and says if he does not arrive home before sundown, he and his horse will both freeze to death."

"Tell him that is no excuse to torture that animal."

"Это не оправдание пытки, что животное," the driver tells the perplexed man.

"Pick up the wheel yourself and allow your cart to freely move," Henry directs with a hand gesture.

The driver translates, "Возьмите колесо себе и позволить вашей корзине свободно передвигаться."

"Or I'll see to it that you will be the one pulling that cart tomorrow," Henry goes on.

"Или я буду следить за тем, что вы будете тянуть одной корзине, что завтра," the driver warns.

Heeding the ambassador's threat, the peasant reluctantly moves to the broken wheel and lifts the axle off the ground. The horse now pulls the cart while the peasant holds up the broken wheel. As the unhappy man and his horse slowly move away, Henry returns to the carriage with a sense of satisfaction. The driver remounts and gives his horses a gentle crack of the reins to continue the journey.

That evening, the Berghs are in their bedroom at the residence provided to them by the Court of St. Petersberg. Matilda is taking her clothes from a large armoire and carefully folding them and putting them into a trunk. Henry is seated, reading the newspaper.

"It will feel good to get home. These Russian winters are much too fierce for a couple of aging gilded lilies like us," Henry declares.

Matilda goes over to her husband and kneels by him affectionately. "You're doing this for me, aren't you? I've taken ill so often since we came here, and you've been so patient with me."

"Now that that dreadful war with the South is over, we can return to Delmonico's for the best steak dinner in New York."

Matilda picks up a piece of paper on the end table. "Is this our travel schedule?"

"Yes. We have official invites to the courts of Spain and England."

"We've never met Queen Isabella," Matilda says. "Is she the Second or Third?"

"The Second," Henry answers. "And her whole Bourbon regime is rife with conflict. I hope she's still queen by the time we arrive in Spain."

"Tell me about her husband," Matilda asks.

"Francis, the Duke of Cadiz. They're double cousins, you know. I'm told he's a homosexual, even though they have a brood of children."

"Really?"

"The rumor is they're not all his. Not that it's any concern of ours."

"And will we see Victoria in England?" Matilda inquires.

"I'm afraid so," Henry answers sarcastically.

"What is it about that woman you don't like?"

"Oh, I don't know. She has the complexion of a boiled lobster and a personality to match." He turns and smiles impishly.

"She can't help her complexion, Henry." There is a pause before they both begin to laugh. Henry loves the way his wife disarms him, and the warm embrace that follows is a nice moment, but it does not substitute for the couple's lack of intimate relations that Henry misses.

The next day the Berghs go to the train station, where they board a deluxe sleeper car that will take them across the European continent. The five-day journey will include eating in the dining car, conversing with other passengers in the club car, Henry writing in his journal, Matilda knitting and much reading. Henry is fascinated by *The World as Will and Representation* by Arthur Schopenhauer, a German philosopher who writes that our world is driven by a continually dissatisfied will, continually seeking satisfaction. While Henry does not consider himself to be an intellectual, the pursuit of knowledge and happiness quietly consumes him. He considers himself to be infinitely fortunate to be born into privilege and wealth. And yet, he is not truly happy and cannot understand why. His life is already rich with fabulous travel, friends of influence, creature comforts and the curse of being able to think.

On the fourth night of their journey, Henry and Matilda get into their sleeping berths early, Matilda in the lower berth and Henry in the upper. The train will arrive in Madrid in the morning, and they want a good night's rest.

"Henry," Matilda calls up to him.

"Yes?" he responds.

"Could you come down and stay with me until I fall asleep?"

"Are you sure?"

"Yes."

Henry does so, lying next to his wife on the outside of the berth. He caresses her with one hand awkwardly meandering across her cheek, down her neck and then on to her breast. He does so with trepidation, as he knows how his wife feels about sexual intercourse. Henry is a big man and the act is painful for her, so their sexual relations have never been successful. Nonetheless, tonight Mr. Bergh will satisfy his wife with the probing strokes of his hand. Matilda is thankfully receptive to Henry's efforts. But Henry eventually returns to his upper berth without his own needs being met. Sleep will eventually end the mixed emotions of the heart and mind.

The morning arrival in Madrid is late and leaves little time for the Berghs to travel to their hotel and leisurely unpack, as they are to meet Spanish royalty to view the national sport of bullfighting, an event neither of the Berghs has experienced in person.

Henry and Matilda are escorted from their hotel by Ricardo Fema, the American attaché to the court of Spain, to the Plaza del Toros in Madrid, an outdoor stadium that is surrounded by a teeming throng of humanity milling about, selling wares and food and lining up to see the spectacle inside the stadium. There is every stratum of Spaniard present, from the well-dressed gentlemen escorting their parasol-carrying ladies to the peasant families of a half dozen little ones being corralled by their harried parents. The Berghs are led through this melange of citizenry to a small guarded entrance, where they are ushered inside as privileged guests. The arena is filled with enthusiastic Spaniards cheering for a line of handsome, young toreadors as they make their entrance, parading proudly in their colorful costumes. Henry and Matilda take in the color and pageantry with the wide eyes of the neophytes they are to such spectacle as they look around the expansive arena. An orchestra at ringside plays as the crowd cheers on each toreador with unbridled enthusiasm as they proudly enter the ring.

Queen Isabella and her husband, Francis, the Duke of Cadiz, are seated in the royal box, viewing the proceedings as Henry and Matilda arrive. Mr. Fema brings the Berghs to the royal couple and introduces them. Henry and Matilda greet the queen and her husband with great respect, bowing and curtsying and greeting them with Spanish phrases they memorized the day before. Isabella seems pleased to have the Americans as her guests. The duke seems more interested in the march of the participants taking place down in the ring. Mr. Fema then takes the Berghs to their seats near the royal couple.

"Tell me, Mr. Bergh, is this your first bullfight?" Fema asks.

"Yes. It's a curious event, isn't it? We all come out in a public arena to watch a man combat a bull? It harkens back to the Roman gladiators, doesn't it?"

Fema replies, "Spaniards don't see it like that. It's a noble contest between man and beast celebrated as an art, much like the dance."

Down in the bullring, the contest is about to begin. With a flourish of horns, the first matador steps forward as the others leave the ring in preparation for the release of the bull. He swirls his cape with a flourish and faces the royal box, then bows in respect to his queen. The crowd cheers enthusiastically. He then turns and walks to the center of the ring and faces the doors where the bull is held. The young matador stares intensely, and there is a long pause as he waits for the release of the bull.

The crowd becomes hushed, as peasants and royalty alike eagerly await the meeting of man and bull. Henry and Matilda are also eager for the game to begin,

looking around the stadium with great interest. The
event is a cultural phenomenon as much as it is a
contest.

On the left side of the bullring, the wooden gates
open and a bull charges into the ring, confused and
agitated. The crowd begins to cheer, and the matador
ruffles his cape cautiously to attract the bull's attention.
The dance between man and beast jogs back and forth
as the bull charges the matador, and he steps aside
quickly to avoid being struck, waving his cape over the
bull's head. This provocative choreography repeats itself
as the crowd cheers.

Three sword-wielding picadors enter the ring and
start circling the bull while waving their swords at him.
As the bull turns to avoid or attack them, one after
another, each one sticks his sword in the bull's neck,
drawing the first blood of the contest. The matador
continues to follow the bull, taunting him with his cape.
The blood seems to enthuse the crowd.

Matilda is visibly shaken by the bloody episode.
Henry seems incredulous that this is occurring and
focuses on observing the bloodthirsty spectators around
him with great interest. The duke is attentive, but the
queen seems blasé about the event, as she hands off her
empty wine glass to an underling to be refilled.

But now, two banderilleros on horseback enter the
ring, circling man and beast from two sides. The bull is
distracted by the horses and snorts and charges in many
directions. The matador runs toward the bull waving his
cape. As the bull turns to charge him, a banderillero
rides by and throws a banderilla, a sharp, barbed stick
with a colorful decoration, into the bull's shoulder. The
bull is angered at the attack as blood runs down his
shoulder with the banderilla stuck in him. The
banderilla flails about as the injured bull bolts and
charges. This assault repeats itself when the second
banderillero on horseback throws a second banderilla

into the bull's other shoulder, drawing more blood from the angry beast.

The matador continues to wave his cape to draw the bull's attention. As the first banderillero rides by again, the bull turns quickly and charges the horse, goring him brutally. The crowd is stunned. The fatally injured horse falls to the ground, throwing off its rider several yards away, who quickly gets up and runs to the ring doors where he hastily exits the arena.

While the royal couple take the events in stride, Matilda begins weeping into a handkerchief with her head turned away from the bull ring. Henry attempts to console her as he keeps one eye on the bullring while taking her into his arms.

With a dead horse lying in the ring, the picadors continue to circle the bull from all directions. One of them hands a large sword to the matador, who then approaches the bull head-on while waving his cape and drawing the sword back ready to make the kill. The bull charges him, but is too fast for the matador to stab with his sword. The men scurry about to reposition themselves as the blood-drenched bull circles angrily.

Now the bull seems a bit dazed. He stops and snorts, shaking his torso wracked with pain. The noise of the crowd dies down a bit, in anticipation of the final showdown. The bull digs his front hooves into the dirt and makes a run for the cape-waving matador. This time the matador moves quickly to the side and thrusts the sword into the bull's neck as it passes. The bull is mortally wounded as it stumbles about, drenched in blood. The crowd responds with applause overtaking the cheers. The bull is about to die as the men form a wide circle around him. With one last breath, the bull collapses. The crowd's applause rises.

The royal couple seem pleased, while Matilda's head is bowed to avoid viewing the bloody spectacle. Henry is now looking on with disgust, but attempting to disguise his contempt as he is a guest of the queen. Matilda turns and whispers to Henry, who then turns to Fema.

"Is there someone who can escort my wife back to our hotel? She's not feeling well."

"Of course, Ambassador Bergh." Fema addresses an aide of his sitting to his left. The aide rises. Henry and Matilda rise, and Henry hands off Matilda to the aide who escorts her from the royal box. Henry and Fema sit back down.

"Señor Fema, tell me, what do you think of all this? I mean your personal feelings about fighting the bulls?"

"As a Spaniard, I recognize the cultural tradition of the spectacle and nobility of the contest. But as a man, frankly, I detest the savagery."

"But you bring visitors here with pride?"

"I am here today because it is my job to be here, and I am loyal to my queen. But do not confuse loyalty with approval."

As the fights continue with new bulls and new matadors, Henry's emotions run the gamut from pity to outrage and from contempt to sadness. His observations of the crowd's cheering approval of the gory event is beginning to have an effect on his stomach, which is usually stoic. But today he is beginning to feel sour.

The last contest of the day ends with the bull goring a picador before being slain. The injured man is taken out on a stretcher as the matador walks to the dead bull, takes out a small knife and cuts off an ear. He then places it in a handkerchief and walks over to the edge of the ring below the royal box and hands the ear to a soldier, who walks it up to the royal box and hands it to the queen, who takes it and hands it over to her husband.

Henry Bergh gets one close-up look at the severed ear and his stomach turns. He rises and makes a hasty exit, to the surprise of Mr. Fema.

The arena's public toilet stalls comprise a long wooden plank with holes in it on which you sit, each stall separated by a wooden divider. Men of various stations in life are urinating, seated and milling about. Henry arrives and makes haste to the first empty stall he sees, where he stoops over the hole in the plank and begins throwing up. As he regurgitates, he thinks to himself how long it's been since something like this has happened. Not since he was a kid, as he recalls, has he vomited with such fervor. But the blood and death of this sport are grotesque and sicken me for a reason, he thinks. Standing up, Henry composes himself and damns the proceedings as barbarism. A spectacular tribute to inhumanity.

Shortly thereafter, Henry leaves the event with Mr. Fema. He declines a carriage and asks Fema to walk with him back to their hotel. The two men walk away from the stadium through the streets of Madrid.

"I'm sorry you and Mrs. Bergh are not feeling well today. I hope your trip to Spain has not been completely unpleasant," Fema apologizes.

"No, but we are anxious to get home to New York and will be leaving for London tomorrow. Tell me, Señor Fema, what is it in the Spanish race that celebrates the brutal death of an animal while the English, for example, would abhor such a spectacle?"

"I guess the English confine their brutality to members of their own species. They don't call it England, Bloody England, for nothing," Fema responds matter-of-factly.

"Yes, that's true," Henry counters, "but the inequity of the fight is what concerns me. The bull, basically, has no chance to survive. Are there no Spaniards that seek to end this blood sport?"

"England has its Royal Society for the Prevention of Cruelty to Animals, but there is nothing like that here."

"I didn't know such a society exists. Do you know much about it?" Henry asks.

"I read an article about it in an English newspaper. I may still have it in my office. Would you like to see it?" Henry responds, "Very much so."

Henry tells Fema that he wants to observe the local color, and the two disappear into the crowded streets of Madrid.

That evening, the Berghs dine with the queen and her husband at the Royal Palace, where no one discusses the day's bloody contests. Henry, through a translator, discusses the recently ended American Civil War, the tragic assassination of his beloved President Lincoln and the issue of slavery, which the queen proudly points out Spain had abolished back in 1811. Despite her stout and dour appearance, for which she is well-known and not particularly popular, Queen Isabella is particularly gracious this evening to Mrs. Bergh and makes sure to include her in the conversation. The royal life is not what people think, she relates to Mrs. Bergh. Matilda, being well-educated, is aware of the struggles Isabella II has endured since ascending to the throne as a three-year-old on her father's passing in 1833, and whose succession was disputed by the opposition Carlist political party. Unfamiliar with Spain's internal politics, Matilda asks the queen about who exactly the Carlists were. Isabella explains Carlism confronted not only the question of who could legitimately sit on the Spanish throne but also the very principles on which Spanish society was built. Should it remain Roman Catholic or should it embrace Enlightenment values? Do governments derive their power from God or do they derive their power from human beings? So when the Carlists refused to recognize a female sovereign, it led to the Carlist Wars, delaying Isabella's formal reign until 1843. Since then, it has been a time of political fragility requiring hard-lined statesmanship, the queen asserts. While the two ladies are worlds apart in every conceivable manner, including their relationships with their husbands, they manage to engage in lively conversation for much of the evening.

Upon retiring to their room, Henry finds the newspaper with the article about the RSPCA, the Royal Society for the Prevention of Cruelty to Animals, in England that Mr. Fema had mentioned. The paper is on the foyer table with a note from Fema. Henry takes it to the bedroom; the couple undress and get ready for bed.

Once comfortable, Henry reads the article aloud to Matilda with the enthusiasm of a schoolboy reciting his newly learned multiplication tables. The organization's mission is to pass laws to protect animals from abusive treatment and cruel conditions and prosecute the offenders. How virtuous is that?

Henry is beginning to compare European and American cultures with a critical eye. Why did America have to fight a war to abolish slavery when Spain, England and many other countries abolished it peacefully decades ago? The formation of a society in England to protect animals from abuse more than four decades ago seems particularly enlightened compared to where American sensibilities presently stand.

Henry informs his wife that their stay in England will be extended for enough time to procure an appointment to visit the RSPCA and speak with its leaders. Matilda sees a side of her husband she hasn't seen in years. He is reinvigorated and filled with motivation and enthusiasm. "It's as if he aged backwards," she thinks. Henry reaches over and extinguishes the flame of the oil lamp on the bed table and kisses his wife goodnight.

CHAPTER 3

Mid-nineteenth century London in the times of Charles Dickens, Robert Browning, George Eliot and even Prussian expatriate Karl Marx was the most populous city in the world. "When a man is tired of London, he is tired of life," wrote Samuel Johnson. Coffeehouses became the centers for political debate. Art, music, nightlife and commerce grew exponentially in the so-called Industrial Revolution, when newfangled mechanical wonders were popping up to change the face of agriculture, manufacturing, mining and transportation. There was also growing awareness and concern for social justice issues, including how humans treat the panoply of domestic, food and work animals that populate the homes, streets and slaughterhouses, known as abattoirs, where many Londoners unknowingly benefited from their suffering.

The Society for the Prevention of Cruelty to Animals was founded in 1824 by a group of twenty-two reformers led by Richard Martin MP, William Wilberforce MP and the Rev. Arthur Broome. It was granted its royal status by Queen Victoria in 1840 to become the RSPCA. The first notable prosecution under the 1822 Martin's Act for cruelty to animals occurred in August 1838 with the trial of Bill Burns, after Burns was found beating his donkey. The prosecution was brought by Richard Martin, MP for Galway, also known as "Humanity Dick," and the case became memorable because he brought the donkey into court.

The RSPCA lobbied Parliament throughout the nineteenth century, resulting in a number of new laws. The Cruelty to Animals Act 1835 amended Martin's Act and outlawed baiting. In 1876, another act was passed to control animal experimentation, given the growing popularity among doctors of vivisection, the practice of performing surgeries on living animal subjects. Despite lacking police powers, the uniformed RSPCA inspectors were powerful symbols to an unwitting public that they had best not abuse dumb animals, as they were called, or be subject to prosecution.

This new British awareness of the rights of animals would culminate in 1894 with the publication of *Animals' Rights: Considered in Relation to Social Progress* by Henry Salt, who is credited with being the first writer to argue explicitly in favor of animal rights. Salt reasons, "If we are ever going to do justice to the lower races, we must get rid of the antiquated notion of a 'great gulf' fixed between them and mankind, and must recognize the common bond of humanity that unites all living beings in one universal brotherhood."

The Berghs arrived from ship's port in Southampton to the beehive of activity that was London. The streets were filled with horse-drawn coaches, pushcarts, pedestrians, children running about and a variety of animals, including dogs, cats, pigs and sheep, roaming wild on a daily basis. From the comfort and security of her coach seated next to her husband, Matilda observes her surroundings through the coach window with the wide-eyed face of an adolescent. Henry is focused on scribbling into his diary, oblivious to the outside world.

"Do you think London will be gay this Christmas?" Matilda asks.

"I would guess," Henry responds without looking up from his writing.

"Is that your diary?"

"Yes. I'm writing about our day at the bullfights."

Matilda winces. "A dreadful sport. I couldn't watch."

"They call it a sport when it's nothing but wicked butchery," Henry looks up and and adds, "After you left that day, I saw four bulls killed and nine horses, all to the cheers of a delighted audience. And both males and females. The Plaza de Toros was filled with a large proportion of woman. Did you notice?"

"Yes, the ladies were beautifully dressed, I'm sure you noticed."

"Never have I experienced a similar degree of disgust or held such contempt for a people calling themselves civilized and at the same time Christians." He stares out the window slowly shaking his head.

Matilda notices his state of contemplation and is puzzled. "Henry?"

Henry turns to his wife. "I'm not a young man any more, Matilda. My plays are not successful."

"You write plays about difficult subjects, Henry. A man who passes as his own son to win the love of a younger woman is perhaps more than theater-going audiences are ready for."

"Shakespeare could have written such a plot. I know I'm no Shakespeare, but I feel as if my life's endeavors are just frivolous, and—"

"Well, you are in service to your country. Doesn't that count for something?" Matilda interrupts.

"Yes... but, the British reformers are well ahead of the Americans."

Matilda is quizzical. "Reformers?"

"We live in a world of privilege, Matilda. Do you remember how easy it was for me to stop that peasant from beating his horse back in St. Petersberg?"

"I do."

"One look at my medallions and the poor man feared for his very freedom. That is the power of privilege."

The Berghs arrive at Brown's Hotel between Dover and Albemarle streets in the Mayfair section, where they unpack and rest for an evening of theater. Henry had heard of the curious and bizarre popularity of a canine drama on the London stage in which the dog rang a doorbell, carried a lantern, dug up a grave and pursued a murderer. *The Dog of Mogaris* was a popular success a few years back. Based upon its reputation, Henry had procured tickets to the latest stage production at the Surrey Theatre of *Dick Whittington*, moreover titled, *Dick Whittington and His Cat; Or, Harlequin Beau Bell, Gog and Magog, and the Rats of Rat Castle*, by Frank Green with music by Sidney Davis. It starred the comedian Arthur Williams, Miss Topsy Venn was Dick, Master David Abrahams was the cat and the Harlequinade featured Tom Lovell as Clown. *Dick Whittington and His Cat* was a seventeenth-century English folk tale that had been used over the years as the basis for a variety of stage pantomimes and other adaptations. Henry had read the story as a child, so when he learned of this current production, he wired the embassy to purchase tickets on his behalf.

Henry's love of the theater is deeply rooted in his cultural and personal life. After attending the very enjoyable production with his wife that evening, one that was filled with whimsy and laughter reacting to the stage antics of the clever and talented actors, he can't help feel a sense of emptiness at the end of the night and grows introspective. He views the playwright as bearing his soul to the world, as he himself has done, albeit unsuccessfully, for most of his adult years. But he wonders what impact stage stories have beyond being fleeting entertainments. What do theater audiences bring home with them after listening to the playwright's message? Can a stage play change the world? Aristophanes wrote *Lysistrata* in 400 B.C., in which the women of Greece withhold sex from their husbands and lovers as a means of forcing the men to stop making war, a beautifully executed strategy that women could easily follow in the real world, but they don't and war still exists. We can find everything we need to know about human nature and how to live in Shakespeare, but we continue to make the same mistakes. Such thoughts are swirling around in Henry's head in an onslaught of confusion, self-doubt and questioning of values instilled in him from youth. Is his lack of religious faith leading him through this empty existence? And then Shakespeare's words from *As You Like It* come to mind, "All the world's a stage, And all the men and women merely players. They have their exits and their entrances, And one man in his time plays many parts, His acts being seven ages." Yes, these words apply to himself, Henry thinks, and for the first time in his life, Henry feels a sense of destiny to move on to the next stage in his life, where his existence will have a new purpose.

The next day would be a life-altering one. When Henry Bergh's coach arrives at a brick building with a bronze plaque reading "RSPCA—The Royal Society for the Prevention of Cruelty to Animals," Henry and Matilda are greeted by a dapper middle-aged gentleman with blond pork-chop sideburns. He is president of the society, Dudley Ryder, the Second Earl of Harrowby, who graciously escorts the Berghs to his office, where the earl invites Henry and Matilda to sit.

"Your Lordship, thank you for seeing us on such short notice," Henry says.

"It is my honor, Ambassador and Mrs. Bergh."

"If you don't mind, please call me Henry and my wife Matilda. We are New Yorkers not in the habit of using official titles," Henry implores.

"Excellent. You need not address me as Your Lordship or Earl of Harrowby. I am Dudley." Crossing to his desk, he continues, "I understand you have a deep compassion for the welfare of animals, Henry."

"Well, it's more of a growing awareness of how cruelly we treat them and why neither the church nor the politicians speak out against such barbarism."

"Our founder, Richard Martin, whom we affecttionately call Humanity Dick, arrived at the same conclusion. One of his profound moments came after

viewing the illustrations of William Hogarth. Let me
share them with you. They are over here."

Ryder rises and crosses to the wall where there are
four framed black and white engravings displayed. He
beseeches the Berghs to follow him for a closer look, and
they comply.

"The set is called 'The Four Stages of Cruelty.' The
pictures are moral lessons depicting four stages in the
life of a fictional boy named Tom Nero." He then directs
them to the first illustration.

"Beginning with 'The First Stage of Cruelty,' the boy
is torturing a dog by inserting an arrow into its rectum
while the other boys assist; the more tender-hearted
boy, perhaps the dog's owner, pleads with them to stop
tormenting the frightened animal. Note the other
cruelties by the other boys in the background to a bird, a
cat, another dog and a cock." (*See illustration 5.*)

He then takes a step to his left. "We move to the
second picture," as Henry and Matilda look on in
fascination. "In 'The Second Stage of Cruelty,' Tom Nero
has grown up and become a hackney coachman, and the
recreational cruelty of the schoolboy has turned into the
professional cruelty of a man at work. Tom's horse,
mistreated and overloaded, has collapsed, breaking its
leg and upsetting the carriage. The corpulent barristers
emerging from the carriage seem merely annoyed at the
inconvenience." (*See illustration 6.*)

Henry and Matilda view the picture with wonder-
ment as well as distress.

He takes another step over. "In the third picture
Tom has turned to robbery, seduction and murder. This
one is called 'Cruelty in Perfection.'" (*See illustration 7.*)

Henry and Matilda both view the picture with
frowns, shaking their heads.

Then they move to the last picture. "Finally, in 'The
Reward of Cruelty,' Tom receives what Hogarth warns
is the inevitable fate of those who start down the path

he has followed: his body is taken from the gallows after his execution as a murderer and is mutilated by surgeons in the anatomical theatre." (*See illustration 8.*) "Extraordinary," Henry exclaims shaking his head.

The earl explains, "The printing and distribution of Hogarth's prints led to The Anatomy Act in 1832, ending the dissection of murderers. Most of the animal tortures depicted were outlawed by the Cruelty to Animals Act in 1835. Our society has used that law to prosecute more than six hundred offenders in our forty years of existence."

"Can I get a printed copy of this law?" Henry asks.

"Why, yes, of course."

"And the society's Articles of Incorporation and By-laws?" Henry continues.

"It will be my pleasure."

They turn and cross to the earl's desk to continue a discussion of animal cruelty issues that lasts more than three hours. By day's end, the Berghs are exhausted, but Henry is now convinced that he has a mission.

"Mrs. Bergh, you are married to the future president of the *American* Society for the Prevention of Cruelty to Animals," he announces on his way to wash up for bed.

"Do you really mean that, Henry?"

From the bathroom Henry calls to her, "I do. This is too important to wait any longer. It's time for America to catch up with the rest of the world."

Back in Mary Ellen Schutt's sunroom, the elderly Mary Ellen adjusts herself in the chair as the filming continues. She recounts, "If Henry Bergh had not met with the Earl of Harrowby in London that winter, I doubt if I would even be here today to tell you any of this."

Her interviewer, Allen Waggoner, follows up, "Tell me the connection."

Mary Ellen continues, "Well, Mr. Bergh had both wealth and friends in high places."

Illus. 3 - MP Richard "Humanity Dick" Martin

Illus. 4 - the trial of Bill Burns, August 1838

The Four Stages of Cruelty
by William Hogarth (1697-1764)

Illus. 5 - First stage of cruelty

Illus. 6 - Second stage of cruelty

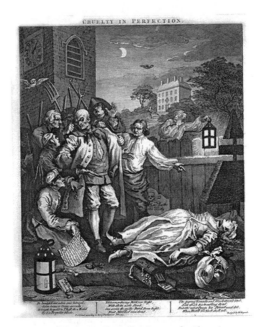

Illus. 7 - Cruelty in perfection

Illus. 8 - The reward of cruelty

CHAPTER 4

On the evening of February 8, 1866, Henry Bergh is scheduled to deliver his first public lecture on animal protection, hoping to drum up enough support to go to the New York State legislature with a charter for an organization replicating England's RSPCA. It's a snowy night, but the weather has not kept the likes of Bergh's influential friends and acquaintances from attending.

Clinton Hall is at the triangle of Astor Place, East Eighth Street and Lafayette Street in Manhattan and is the home to the Mercantile Library of New York, the fourth largest library in the United States, exceeded in size only by the Library of Congress, the Boston Public Library and the Astor Library, which later became the New York Public Library. The building is named after Dewitt Clinton, who was mayor of New York City from 1803 to 1815 and governor of New York State from 1817 to 1823 and again from 1825 to 1828. Among his achievements, Clinton was instrumental in the creation of the Erie Canal, which became nicknamed "Clinton's Ditch." As the Federalist presidential candidate in 1812, he lost the election to James Madison. Clinton was also an acquaintance of Henry's father, who was opposed to Clinton's politics but respectful of his office.

The Mercantile Library's public reading room accommodates a couple hundred guests. At seven p.m., the room is brightly gaslit with large chandeliers and about two-thirds filled when New York City Mayor John T. Hoffman enters with his entourage. He is greeted respectfully by the others in attendance as he makes his way to an aisle seat a few rows from the makeshift stage, where a lectern is placed for Henry Bergh's use.

Frank Leslie, the editor of the popular weekly *Illustrated Newspaper,* sporting his distinguished gray goatee and a steno pad, approaches the mayor, bends down and offers his hand. "Good evening, Mayor Hoffman."

"Mr. Leslie, nice to see you. Are you here to support our friend, Henry Bergh?"

"I'm here to cover his lecture for my paper. Mr. Bergh has become quite outspoken on behalf of reforming our way with animals. That's of interest to both myself and my readers."

"Yes, I understand Mr. Bergh is proposing new laws to protect the dumb beasts from the smart ones."

The audience begins to applaud as Henry Bergh takes the stage and steps up to a wooden lectern. He has shaved his sideburns and appears younger and more invigorated. Leslie excuses himself and takes his seat, as the audience applauds politely.

After introducing himself, Bergh begins. "Man's brutality toward animals goes back to the beginning of time. Today, we fancy ourselves a civilized society, but right here in the streets of New York occurring on a daily basis is the beating, the overloading and the underfeeding of the horses that pull our wagons and streetcars. Despicable and unsanitary conditions exist at our dairy barns, and barbarous means of carrying animals from the farms to the abattoirs where savage methods of killing these beasts takes place. The sportsmen engage in dogfighting, cockfighting, hunting and ratting with a callousness that lacks all notions of earthly compassion. And now there are doctors in France who engage in scientific experimentation on animals by dissecting them alive. Such vivisectors, as they are called, wish to bring this brutal practice to this country. Where does the evil man perpetrates end? Who is there to say, 'Enough?'"

Henry speaks for almost thirty minutes, and the elegance and passion with which he lays out a case to formalize the protection of animals are compelling. Some members of his audience must wipe tears from their eyes on hearing for the first time the cruelty and conditions animals endure at the hands of humans. Many are eager to get on the bandwagon, so when Henry finishes, he leaves the stage to press the flesh with his audience and finds respect and enthusiasm. With him, he carries his petition.

That evening, Henry Bergh collected the signatures of twenty-five of the most influential New Yorkers on his petition for a proposed animal protection society charter that Bergh calls a Declaration of Independence.

Wasting no time, Henry immediately begins his campaign in earnest to get one hundred prominent signatures on his petition that he will take to Albany. First, he wants his SPCA charter, which would include the police powers lacking in England's RSPCA, and then he wants laws to protect animals codified, so that America, or at least New York, will lead the way in reforming the treatment of domestic, work and food animals. Henry and Matilda send invitations to a series of receptions at their home in which Henry can personally entertain and lobby those who can help him bring credibility to his cause by having them sign on as supporters.

The Fifth Avenue townhouse of Mr. and Mrs. Henry Bergh is a well-appointed one and becomes the headquarters of Henry's campaign. On this evening, servants are putting out food and drink at a dinner party populated by a couple dozen well-heeled guests. Matilda is greeting guests as they arrive when Henry enters from the study holding a parchment scroll. He crosses the room to greet Elbridge T. Gerry, a dapper, middle-aged gent sporting salt and pepper pork-chop sideburns. Gerry is a longtime confidant of Henry's and his personal attorney. Gerry is well-connected and one of the smartest, well-regarded lawyers in New York.

"Here it is, Elbridge. Signed by seventy-five of the most prominent New Yorkers, and tonight Peter Cooper and the Roosevelt brothers will sign, and we can present this to the legislature by week's end."

"Will this be the last of these dinner parties?"

"For now," Henry responds. "It's cost me a small fortune but well worth it."

"How much have you spent promoting this effort, Henry?"

"Leave it to my lawyer to be looking out for my finances. Likely more than $15,000. But I'd spend double that if that's what's required to get our charter and pass our bill."

Gerry looks across the room, "There's Mr. and Mrs. Cooper. Let me greet them and I will bring them to you."

"Very good."

Gerry exits and Henry walks to a distinguished-looking man sporting a turned-up mustache and a monocle.

"Dr. Pachtman, it's good to see you again."

"Henry, your home is becoming an epicenter for the good-hearted," Pachtman says as he cleans his pince-nez glasses with a hankie.

"We should not be the exception because of our positions in society, don't you think?" Henry responds.

"I think you have an uphill battle, as the generals say. The great unwashed notwithstanding, there are still many of my colleagues who resent your public statements opposing their vivisectors. How do you plan to sway this group of infidels?"

"For one, I do not see them as infidels, but rather as the loyal opposition. I'll debate them directly on their own turf. That is the way of the academics, is it not?

"It is."

Henry continues, "But first, I must have the legal authority, not merely claim the moral authority, to impose this new standard. That's why these gatherings are not just high teas for the ladies."

Pachtman laughs, "I have faith in you, my boy."

A heavy-set woman with blonde curls and a collection of emerald jewelry to complement her pea-green dress is chatting with Matilda. "I must tell you that if my husband does not sign your husband's petition, I will personally take his hand and lead it to the inkwell."

"Thank you, Mrs. Asbury."

"We read the text of Mr. Bergh's address at Clinton Hall in the *Globe,* and we were shocked to learn of this problem," she gushes.

"It is a hidden problem in many cases," Matilda answers.

"Indeed," Mrs. Asbury coos. "If people only knew!"

"Henry has often said that if the slaughterhouse walls were made of glass, there would be a lot more vegetarians."

"Oh yes, that's a wonderful quote. I will use that at the next D.A.R. meeting."

"Thank you," Matilda replies, "Getting the word out is so important."

After an hour of cocktails and conversation that has given Matilda, Henry and Elbridge an opportunity of socializing one-to-one, Henry moves around the room ringing a little bell to get everyone's attention. When the guests quiet down, he asks that everyone move to chairs arranged in the parlor so he can speak more formally to them for a moment. The guests migrate to the next room where all take seats arranged facing the fireplace. Henry thanks his guests for cooperating and walks to the front of the gathering, standing in front of the fireplace facing them. He greets them again and tells them he has just a few words he would like to impart.

"Last summer was one of the worst I have ever seen for the welfare of New York City's horses. On the average, we saw a horse a week drop dead in the streets from a lack of water and a lack of common sense by their owners. These poor beasts pull our carts and carriages, and our overcrowded streetcars, and we reward them with a bucket of hay and a crack of the whip. They die in the streets to the horror of our women and children. And it does not have to continue. It is time to legislate a more humane society with our SPCA."

The crowd politely applauds.

"On Friday we will take our society's charter and our animal cruelty bill to Albany and, thanks to your support, begin the long process of teaching people that the dumb animals, be they the horse, the dog or cat, or even the lowly rat, are due at least our respect, if not our kindness."

The elder Roosevelt brother speaks, "The teamsters and the owners of the abattoirs will oppose you, Henry. Not to mention the streetcar companies and the sport hunters."

"You forgot the vivisectors, Mr. Roosevelt," Henry adds. Some laughter breaks out.

"Thanks to all of you in this room, and other like-minded souls, I am confident we will prevail in Albany. At least, that is the opinion of my lawyer, whose judgment I should perhaps suspect, as he never sends me a bill." More laughter affirms Henry's ability to charm the crowd.

Illus. 9 - left, Henry Bergh, right, Elbridge T. Gerry

Illus. 10 - Frank Leslie illustrates the need for an SPCA in 1865:
"City Enormities—Every Brute Can Beat His Beast."

CHAPTER 5

The elderly Mary Ellen has been sitting stoically for some time now, telling the story about which she is so passionate. Her mildly arthritic hips are in need of an adjustment in the chair, so she stops and moves for her comfort.

"We can take a break, if you like," Allen, her interviewer, says sympathetically.

"No, that's all right," Mary Ellen replies. "This is a very comfortable chair and sometimes I'm in it reading for hours before I realize how much time has passed."

She takes a sip from the glass of iced tea next to her and then continues.

"In a matter of days after traveling to Albany with Mr. Gerry, Mr. Bergh got his charter for America's first animal protection society and less than two weeks after that the state legislature passed the first law in America to protect animals from the kind of cruelty that was pretty much commonplace and accepted up to that time. And it also gave Mr. Bergh's society police powers to enforce the new law."

Mary Ellen grows suddenly animated as she tells the story. "It was an extraordinary achievement. I mean, it was only a year after the end of the Civil War, but Mr. Bergh was then faced with getting the word out that such law existed."

"How did he do that?" her interviewer asks.

Mary Ellen smiles broadly.

Henry Bergh wastes no time in setting up shop for his new enterprise when he rents two attic rooms at Broadway and Fourth Street, furnished with what he tells his wife is "the very plainest kind of kitchen furniture" to run the day-to-day operations of the society. When some of his friends and supporters ridiculed the dingy quarters and hard wooden chairs his staff would be sitting in to do their work, Henry insisted, "I'm not wasting money on frills when we have an important mission to carry out. If it's a matter of a comfortable sofa or hiring an enforcement agent, I'll hire the agent and sit on a hard chair. That's just simple logic."

Amid the hustle and bustle of nineteenth-century New York City are the street vendors, wagons drawn by horses, carts drawn by dogs, free-roaming cats, dogs and farm animals, as well as children running in the streets forming a sometimes chaotic melange of urban activity. It is Henry's mission to begin patrolling the streets, seek out cruelties in plain view and cite the lawbreakers in a very public manner to gain the most public exposure for the society's activities.

Henry and one of his uniformed agents named Gus emerge from the new headquarters past a small wooden sign at the ground floor entrance on which Mrs. Bergh had painted the letters "A.S.P.C.A." and the words "American Society for the Prevention of Cruelty to Animals, 4th floor," and that he had personally affixed to the building. Henry is dressed in his long formal overcoat and top hat and sports his newly-minted ASPCA shield on one lapel.

"Gus, we have only a dozen men to police the entire city," Henry says. "That means we must focus our efforts on the most public of infractors and set an example for the rest."

"I've looked into the Sportsman's Hall, as you asked, Mr. Bergh, and it's a hotbed of dogfighting and ratbaiting almost every night. The proprietor is a notorious little varmint named Kit Burns," Gus tells his boss.

"Yes, I've heard of Mr. Burns. He appears to rule Water Street without a gang. We'll get a warrant and pay him a visit."

As they are speaking, and having not even walked a full city block, across the street they observe a man who has just finished loading barrels onto a horse-drawn cart. The barrels are too heavy for the lone horse to pull as the man whips the horse mercilessly to get him to move. The horse is struggling unsuccessfully to move the heavy cart and whinnies as the aggressive driver whips him. On seeing the scene, Henry clenches his jaw and indicates for Gus to follow him as he crosses the street and approaches the man.

"You there! You'll have to unload some of those barrels. No horse could pull such a load," Henry calls out.

The driver looks at the tall stranger in formal attire and is not impressed. "Mind your business."

Henry flashes his badge and moves closer. "I order you to stop in the name of the law."

The driver looks Henry up and down and replies, "You're the law? In a pig's eye," and he continues to whip the horse, which struggles to move the heavy load forward just a few inches.

Henry gestures to Gus, who grabs the whip and pulls the man from his seat on the cart down to the ground. The driver is furious and gets up ready to throw a punch at Gus, who takes a defensive stance, raising his fists. In the meantime, Henry has gone to the back of the cart and when the driver looks over, he sees Henry knocking barrels off the end of the cart. He runs over to him.

"Hey now, I'm gonna—"

"You're gonna what?" Henry interrupts. And with that Henry takes a folded paper from his inside pocket and hands it to the driver.

"What's this?" the driver asks.

"A summons. You'll appear in court to explain to the judge why you overload your cart and beat your horse in violation of the state anticruelty law. Now take off half of those barrels or I'll have my officer take you to jail with dispatch."

The driver is speechless.

The City of New York, as most of America, is rife with indifference and cruelty when it comes to work animals, particularly the horses that do all the hauling. But domestic animals also suffer unbelievable fates. One has to walk only a few blocks before a situation exploiting or harming an animal could be seen.

Merely a day after Henry cited the driver pulling too many barrels, Henry and another of his agents named Billy leave the office and are walking toward the docks to investigate a report of dogfighting when they are spotted by a woman who is agitated and running frantically down the street.

The woman sees the uniformed agent and is elated. "Officer, please. You must come with me. The man won't stop what he's up to. He's around the corner."

"What is he doing, madam?" Henry asks.

"Please, come with me," she implores, dragging him by the sleeve.

Around the corner is a construction site where a worker is bricking a wall from a short scaffold. The woman arrives with Henry and Officer Billy and points out the wall that is rising to a height of three-quarters of a story.

"That's where it is. I heard it with my own ears. There's a cat in that wall and he's about to seal it in there alive," the woman accuses.

Henry gets the picture and steps forward and calls out to the worker, "You, sir. Stop your work and come down here."

The worker looks over confusedly, "What? What for?"

"This lady tells me there is a cat trapped behind that wall," Henry calls out to him.

"What if there is?" the worker responds arrogantly.

Henry steps closer. "I order you to stop your work or be taken into custody."

Henry flashes his badge and Agent Billy steps forward to back him up. The worker begrudgingly hops down to the ground and approaches Bergh. While this scene unfolds, a crowd of passersby and neighborhood locals begin to form to observe the confrontation.

The burly worker gives Bergh the once-over, noticing his fancy clothes. "All right, Governor," he spews sarcastically. "What can I do for you today?"

"You can tear down that wall and release the cat that's inside," Henry responds with authority.

The worker isn't impressed. "Mister, I ain't busting up two days' work for a mangy old alley cat."

Henry holds his ground. "Yes, you will."

"Yeah? And just who says so?"

Henry takes a step forward. "I do," he says with steely resolve.

When the worker defiantly does not respond, Henry steps forward and gets into the worker's face. "The law protects that animal and I'm here to see that the law is obeyed."

The worker is having none of this. Suddenly, he reaches back to take a swing at Henry, but instantly Henry sucker punches him in the belly before the worker can strike. The worker doubles over. Henry is turning to Agent Billy when the worker unexpectedly swings around and hits Henry in the side, knocking him to the ground.

The crowd that has gathered begins to get excited. Billy grabs the worker as Henry recovers and gets back up. Henry dusts off his top hat and approaches the worker, who Billy is now restraining.

"Let him go," Henry orders Billy, who releases the angry man.

"Now I'm going to ask you only once. Will you take down the wall sufficient to liberate the cat? Or shall I have my officer take you into custody for cruelty to animals?"

The man looks at the uniformed agent and at the badge on Henry's lapel and is burning but defeated. "What a country," he mutters as he skulks away and picks up a sledgehammer to begin undoing his work on the wall.

Henry gestures to the woman to follow the worker to retrieve the cat. She is elated and looks at Henry Bergh as if Jesus himself had returned to save feline souls.

"Bless you, Mister—"

"Bergh. Henry Bergh."

"Bless you, Mr. Bergh."

Henry Bergh's public campaign to fight animal cruelty and abuse took to the streets of New York with the swiftness and energy of a new conquering army. There was no shortage of missions in Henry Bergh's purview. Despite hiring a staff of a dozen agents who had official peace officer status, giving them the power to arrest and issue summonses to appear in court, he became obsessed with personally intervening.

On one busy street filled with pushcarts, Henry orders the driver of a cart filled with rags being pulled by a dog to unhook the poor animal. When the driver balks, Bergh pulls out a summons and calls for his uniformed officer standing nearby to come forward, now becoming a familiar but effective tactic. As expected, the driver begrudgingly unhooks the dog from the cart and begins pulling the cart himself. And again, a citizen becomes aware of the new anticruelty laws on the books, with the hope he will spread the word to his friends and family.

Henry Bergh and his agents, emboldened by their early successes, wield their sword of authority throughout the city. On another day, two SPCA agents converge on a meat-packing truck overloaded with live cattle. The poor beasts' heads are sticking out from the side slats of the horse-drawn cart, one on top of another. The first agent flashes his badge as he steps in front of the moving truck. The second agent calls out to the driver to stop, which the driver does. Pointing out the overfilled truck, the driver angrily steps down from his cab. Henry Bergh steps into the scene holding the familiar summons and hands it to the driver with a stern warning. The driver points to his company's sign, Metropolitan Meat Co., swearing and gesturing wildly that his bosses won't take this lying down. Henry laughs and tells the driver if they don't like it, they can come and tell it to the court magistrate.

Investigation is crucial to ferreting out where animal cruelty is taking place behind closed doors. As the ASPCA's reputation begins to spread, tips from the public begin to come in through neighbors, workers with a conscience and witnesses who now have somewhere to go to report cruelty. Less than a month after receiving its charter, an anonymous letter arrives at the ASPCA complaining that at the foot of Day Street, chickens were being plucked and plunged into boiling water alive. Henry reads the handwritten letter at ten A.M. and by ten-fifteen leaves with an agent to personally investigate.

Arriving at the location, the two men sneak around the perimeter of the poultry cages, which is bounded by a picket fence. Peering through the wooden slats, they observe a heartbreaking scene of dozens of birds with broken legs and wings hobbling about among dead birds with twisted necks, some with and some without feathers, some thrown into barrels, some lying on the ground waiting to be collected like yesterday's trash.

Henry Bergh's sense of pity for the poor creatures that suffer at the hands of human beings is always a struggle with his outrage at the inhumanity, and this conflict is resolved in his mind with a committed determination to seek justice.

Henry and his agent enter the premises with authority of the law and and cite the owners, two brothers, with multiple summonses and issue a stern warning to clean up the mess and cease and desist handling the birds as if they were without feelings. The owners vow to fight the charges.

The first successful prosecutions by the ASPCA were dealing with mistreatment of horses. Since the courts had yet to deal with ruling on the new anticruelty law regarding most other animals, how a judge would rule was unpredictable. Two weeks after Henry's inspection, a trial in the poultry case takes place before Justice Kelly. Because he is a witness, Henry Bergh is anxious to testify. His testimony is a passionate plea to punish the callous evildoers who torture birds before they die and become tomorrow's dinner. That the creatures are food animals is irrelevant. They are living, sentient beings capable of feeling pain, which the law prohibits humans from inflicting on beasts of any ilk.

The judge listens to the testimony of the brothers that their chickens had been stabbed in the brains before they were plucked, pleading their defense that they are attempting, at the least, to alleviate suffering.

To Henry Bergh's disheartenment, the trial concludes with a ruling in favor of the defendants, as the judge is not only impressed by the brothers' testimony but also as a strict reading of the law, birds are not classified as animals and, therefore, are not protected by the statute.

Outside the court, Henry vents to his attorney, "The judge is unenlightened," he complains.

"I agree," attorney Gerry concurs. "This is a process that is evolving."

"Not quickly enough. The prevailing attitude among legal professionals will require the need for something monstrous to dramatize the plight of abused animals of all species, not just the work animals."

"Perhaps," Mr. Gerry replies.

"Notoriety is the only way to influence the decision-makers in the criminal justice system," Henry later describes as the solution. The poultry decision garnered little attention in the press, and despite losing the case, Henry Bergh quickly decides it will not be the only opportunity to test the legal system's prosecution of animal abuse to other than dogs, cats, horses and cattle.

Mr. Bergh didn't have to wait long to find another opportunity. In reading the morning paper just a few days later, he comes across an announcement of the arrival of the schooner *Active* that is loaded with a shipment of live turtles at a pier in the East River. Minutes later, he gathers the staff for the morning assignment meeting, where he addresses his agents and reads the announcement. He look up and adds, "This is an opportunity to create a sensation that the newspapers will report. At noon today, we will board the ship, inspect the condition of the turtles and if we find abuse, which I'm sure we will, confiscate the cargo and arrest the captain. We need to put the protection of all animals on the map, and turtles are no exception."

Henry strategizes that the best way to make sure newspapers report the turtle raid is to invite reporters to show up and watch. He hands envelopes to four of his agents and directs them to deliver the invites to the editors of four newspapers right away. Checking his pocket watch, Henry returns to his desk to finish reading the newspapers and wait for the noon appointment at the good ship *Active*.

It's a sunny day when Henry Bergh and his dozen agents gather in front of the building ready to travel to the pier some twenty blocks away. Two wagons will take the law enforcement cadre to their destination. The uniformed men load in, and Henry jumps in last with the driver. He is dressed in his signature long coat, gold shield and top hat.

Captain Nehemiah H. Calhoun is a weary traveler, having steered his vessel all the way from Newfoundland to New York harbor. And having docked on time, he was now awaiting the buyer of his cargo to arrive and collect the eighty-six turtles from the ship's hold. A quick rest in Captain's quarters seems like a good way to revive himself, and he heads below deck for his midday rest when he hears shouting from above.

Henry Bergh and his twelve uniformed agents have boarded the ship and demand to see the cargo. The crew gathers ominously around Bergh and his men. The ship's ensign is a lanky redhead with a prominent scar across one cheek, and he insists only the captain can authorize such an inspection. The timing is fortuitous, as Captain Calhoun enters the deck to confront the intruders. Henry flashes his badge and presents his search warrant signed by Magistrate Walters. The captain begrudgingly takes them below.

The hold is dark and damp. Henry orders the portholes opened to let in light. Shallow wooden crates are lined up for the entire length of the ship. The turtles are on their backs, looking half dead with thirst and starvation. Blood is oozing from their fins where holes had been made and rope had been run through them at the outset of the trip to keep the poor creatures from turning back over and moving about.

Henry is shocked at the scene and turns to the captain, "What breed of a man are you to do this?"

The captain is indignant, "I did nothing. The shipper is responsible for how they travel, not me."

"You can tell that to the judge. You're under arrest." Henry walks over to the nearest upside-down turtle and bends in for a closer look. "You should be made to look into the glassy eyes of these poor wretches." Looking up at the captain, "They suffer not just physical pain but mental anguish at the hands of you and your crew." He waves at Agent Gus. "Untie these beauties. We'll take them into the sunlight after we take Captain Calhoun and his men to the Tombs."

The captain and his crew are furious at being corralled against their wishes at gunpoint off the ship. They are cursing and hollering to the crowd of local dock workers who have gathered to witness the arrest and are none too pleased to see their brethren being hauled away to jail. Henry Bergh sees the howling mob developing around the ship and shooes them away, threatening arrest for them, too, if they interfere.

A man with a notepad and pencil approaches Henry, "Mr. Bergh, I'm Fred Stillwell from the *Times*."

"Fred, I'm glad to see you," Henry greets him, breaking from the line of arrestees he is accompanying. "Won't you come below to witness the conditions?"

"Absolutely," he replies, as another man runs up to them out of breath.

"Are you Mr. Bergh?" the man asks.

"I am," Henry answers him.

"Jeremy Shanahan, *New York Observer*. Can you tell me about the charges these men are facing?"

"I can do better. I can show you. Come with me gentlemen."

Henry escorts the two reporters onto the ship to view the turtles in shipment below.

Illus. 11 - ASPCA headquarters at Fourth Avenue
and Twenty-second Street, New York, 1876

Illus. 12 - Henry Bergh's emblem for the ASPCA

Illus. 13 - "Arrested for cruelty" from *Harpers's Weekly*,
January 13, 1872

CHAPTER 6

Henry Bergh makes sure to read the dozen newspapers that are published in New York City every day, scanning the pages for any story that relates to animals. It didn't take long for the press to take notice of him and his society and line up in support of his mission and activities or criticize and often deride him. After all, the ASPCA was sending people to jail and making examples of all kinds of citizens and businesses who were used to enjoying and profiting from their own use of animals. Henry Bergh was becoming a known personality in New York City and a colorful and controversial one at that. And that suits him just fine.

Henry struggles with developing a thick skin, as some newspapers began caricaturing him in cartoons that often had stinging effect of making fun, which went to the heart of Bergh's credibility with the public. And then again, Henry's imposing physical appearance would lend itself to being portrayed as an authority figure, which pleases him.

This morning, Henry spots a cartoon of a giant caricatured man with a walking stick sporting a Henry Bergh name tag bending down over the city of New York reaching for a horse and carriage. The caption reads, "The Great Meddler."

"Look, Gus," Henry holds up the paper.

Agent Gus asks, "Is that *The Observer?*"

"*The Herald*. They're calling me 'The Great Meddler.'"

"I saw the cartoon. I'm sorry, sir."

"Sorry? Don't be sorry, my friend. Be delighted. I couldn't buy this kind of attention. Why, do you realize after a few more of these newspaper accounts of our activities, the entire city will be talking about us?"

With delight, he takes out an envelope and pulls out a letter. "Look at this. A letter from a woman on Duane Street. 'Dear Mr. Bergh. I read about your society and the arrest of a man for beating his horse on Broadway. You are angels sent from heaven. Please accept this small donation toward your good work.'"

He turns over the envelope and a coin spills out. "And there was another one like this just yesterday."

"A few coins, sir?"

"I know it's not a lot of money, but don't you see? It says we're not alone, Gus. They can make fun of us all they like in the papers, but we're not alone."

Along the East River, ragamuffin kids run around, longshoremen are unloading cargo from ships, and horses, dogs, hogs and goats are being chased, pulled and otherwise manhandled by youngsters and workers alike. It's a beehive of activity as Henry and Matilda Bergh walk along the docks by the river, both dressed as the well-to-do folks they are.

"My God this city is changing," Henry observes. "Had we not sold the shipyard, this is where it would still be. Right here."

"That's almost twenty years ago, Henry," Matilda reminds her husband.

Henry shakes his head, "Look at it. A coal yard. Black soot everywhere."

"Look at the bright side, Henry. You sold your father's business to the Westervelts and they almost lost a fortune, not you."

Henry is engrossed in thought, "And these ships carry the animals in and out as if they were any other manufactured good. I should write a play on that subject. Let the theatergoers be informed of the conditions they never see."

"Yes, you should do that, my love."

Henry takes out a lead pencil and a piece of paper and begins to write. "Yes. 'To plead for mercy to the helpless brute; To fight for those who stand defenseless and mute.' I'll make the protagonist of my play a goat. Let him speak the thoughts we never get to hear."

"I think you'll be the first one to write a soliloquy for a goat, my dear."

Henry laughs. "Am I a fool, Matilda?"

She thinks. "How did Shakespeare put it, 'A fool thinks himself to be wise, but a wise man knows himself to be a fool.'"

Henry is pleased by her quote, but suddenly they hear dogs barking frantically and turn to see where the distressed calls are coming from. Ahead of them, they see a large wooden crate with open slats suspended over the river. The barking dogs are inside. The top of the crate is attached by rope with a winch to a tall wooden crane with two men holding the rope. Uniformed city workers are preparing to lower the crate into the river to drown the dogs. With stoic determination, Henry takes Matilda's hand and begins to walk briskly toward the nearest worker.

Henry calls out to the man, "Sir, tell me who you work for."

The worker sees Henry, but is unfazed. "The Board of Health, Mr. Bergh."

"So, you know me?" Henry replies.

"We all know you, Mr. Bergh."

"How often do you fill this cage with the poor strays?"

"Depends on the day's catch," the worker answers. "Usually once, sometimes twice. If it weren't for the hydrophobia epidemic, I'd let them all go myself, if the commissioner wouldn't find out."

"The hydrophobia epidemic ended five years ago," Henry notes.

Filled with pity, the worker asks, "Can't your society do anything to stop this? I have nightmares when I sleep, but I have to feed my family."

"Thank you for your candor. I'm going to make it a point to talk to the commissioner first thing tomorrow. Let's go, Matilda."

The Berghs turn and walk away from a scene they do not wish to observe, when the worker will discharge his duty and lower the cage into the river.

On each night that Henry Bergh retires to bed, his head swirls with the thoughts and challenges and conflicts of the day; and each new day that arrives brings new strategies and actions for Henry Bergh to execute. Sometimes, just getting out of bed can be filled with dread, knowing what the day's activities will entail.

In the morning, Henry is looking in the bathroom mirror, examining his aging face. He touches the bags under his eyes, pulls back the extra skin under his chin and examines the gray hair emerging from his temples. He is a man in his fifties and clearly not happy about it. He then picks up a small bottle containing a dark liquid and pours some on a cotton ball. He dabs the cotton ball onto the gray hair on his temples and forehead, which darkens the hair to match the rest of it.

Henry sees his maid, Marie, in the mirror through the bathroom doorway putting away clothes in the bedroom armoire and calls out to her. "Marie, can you go to the apothecary today? I'm almost out of the walnut juice."

"Yes, Mr. Bergh," the dutiful servant answers.

Henry finishes his hair touch-up, runs a comb across his pate, hitches up his suspenders and returns to the bedroom, where Marie is folding clothes on the bed and putting them away. Henry goes to the tall mirror and proceeds to fix his necktie.

"Thank you, Marie."

The maid is curious. "Mr. Bergh, may I ask you a question?"

"Of course."

She speaks cautiously, "Well, I've worked for you and the missus for almost twenty years, and your new society is a wonderful thing."

"Thank you. What's your question?"

She proceeds, "It's just that we've never had any animals in the house, and I've never observed you around animals, other than the carriage horses."

"That's true. You want to know why I've made it my life's work to stop cruelty to animals?"

"If you don't mind my asking," she states cautiously.

"It's the injustice that offends me," he answers her simply.

She thinks about that and then says. "There is much injustice in the world, Mr. B. We just fought a war over it."

"Is it just that I was born into wealth and you weren't? Perhaps not. But I don't beat you to make you work. And if I did, you could leave. Can you make the same claim for the horse?" Henry goes to the armoire, retrieves and puts on his jacket and turns to leave the room, adding, "Don't forget my walnut juice."

Sportsman's Hall is a tavern on Water Street in lower Manhattan located just south of Peck Slip and just west of the Five Points, and the tavern is quite notorious. The location has a history of illicit activities under a series of unsavory owners. Its present proprietor, Kit Burns, is a stocky Irishman sporting mutton-chop whiskers on a pock-marked face. On a rainy afternoon, he is outside accepting delivery from a beer truck.

"Where's Mr. Porter?" Burns asks the delivery man, as he is not the usual driver.

The driver answers, "I heard he fell down and broke his leg."

"Send him my best regards, will you?" the garrulous Irishman answers.

"Will do, Mr. Burns." He unloads the last barrel and sets it next to the others beside the cellar doors.

"That should hold us through the weekend," Burns tells him.

The driver decides to be chatty. "I live up on Houston Street and I've come here a few nights when there were no dogfights. What's happened? You used to have them almost every night."

Burns answers, "Well, Mr. Bergh's animal society has been breathing down my neck, sending his agents in to find out when we're booked. He thinks he's going to arrest the lot of us, but I'm playing him for a sucker. See, I take out the dogs before dark to make his people think there's a fight that night, and then I make the event on another night. His guys have been here a half dozen times already and each time go home empty-handed." He laughs with self-satisfaction.

"I'd like to come on a good night, if you know what I mean," the driver prods.

"Sure, sure. You come tomorrow night and you won't be disappointed," Burns tells him.

"Tomorrow is payday," the driver adds.

"Well, ain't that perfect," Burns says. He takes a card from his pocket and hands it to the young driver. "You use this and the admission is on me. The wagerin' is yours, though. Good luck, son."

"Thank you kindly, Mr. Burns," the driver answers politely. Burns slaps the boy on the back and returns to his tavern.

Christopher "Kit" Burns was a street tough from Donegal who moved from Brooklyn to Manhattan, running with the gangs of the Five Points through his twenties. In 1866, the same year as the incorporation of the ASPCA, he opens a tavern at No. 273 Water Street and names it Sportsman's Hall. He is known throughout the neighborhood as a friendly barkeep who is fond of his whiskey and kind to working men, but also a ruthless thug who has been known to send his adversaries to the infirmary.

Dogfighting, ratting, cockfighting and other blood sports had been illegal in New York State since 1865, but the pastimes continue to be popular and thrive in the Fourth Ward behind closed doors of taverns, warehouses, dance halls, bucket shops and sailors' boarding houses near the wharf.

The front of Sportsman's Hall is a barroom with heavy oak furniture, the mounted heads of hunting specimens hanging above, pictures of hunting scenes and prints of noted boxers hanging on the walls and a long oak bar with a shiny brass rail just above the floor. Behind the bar is a small wooden door that opens to a narrow passageway to the rear of the building leading to the pit. Here, an amphitheater of seats that can hold two hundred fifty spectators comfortably, but is often packed with as many as four hundred, rises to the ceiling around an oval pit surrounded by a two-foot wall where the competition of various blood sports takes place. The most popular are the jaw-breaking dogfights involving the bulldogs Burns keeps in his basement. Another blood sport is rat-baiting, where a spaniel or terrier is set against fifteen or twenty wharf rats to kill them one by one as the terrified rodents scurry frantically about the pit, trying to burrow into the crevices or scale the wall to escape their bloody end. Other times the rats are starved to ferocity and set against each other. The place is also famous for bear-baiting, where Burns set dogs against a black bear that he keeps in an iron cage in the corner of the basement and takes out only for special occasions. These events are held for enthusiastic crowds of gambling men who view the bloody shows as mere entertainment and a chance to go home with a little extra in their pockets. Kit Burns and his chums take care to keep their illegal amusements secret, well aware of the need for secrecy even though it may diminish business.

Burns offers a hot lunch of roasted poultry, pork or beef, succotash or potatoes, and a variety of puddings or cakes, which the local patrons wash down with beer or stronger drink and then return to their dock jobs, construction sites or pushcarts a bit fatter and slower. It is after lunch that Burns takes out his fighting dogs for walks along the wharf. Today he meets up with a fellow dogfighter named Harry Hill to discuss future contests. Hill is an ex-prizefighter who arrives with his fourteen-year-old nephew.

"Take Neptune, son," Burns hands the rope leash attached to a brindle bulldog to the boy, "so I can handle Charlie. Hold on tight." The boy grabs the leash tightly, looking at his uncle with surprise, as Burns takes out a white bulldog and the three walk toward the wharf, a block to the east.

"So, Kit," Harry Hill says, "I have three new dogs that I can put to work whenever you're ready."

Kit is distracted as he looks around to see if he is being watched. "Yeah, yeah, I'm full up for the month with Jonny Allen's new litter. But first thing next month you can have the weekends and two more weekdays."

"I've read about how they closed down Dick Morgan's place and took him to the Tombs along with forty-five customers," Harry says.

"Yes, that fucker Henry Bergh is on the warpath, and he thinks taking everyone in custody will kill the business. But I heard Judge Dowling got angry when his courtroom was full up with defendants, and he dismissed all the charges except for Dick's."

"Bergh is a meddling fucker, all right."

"Well, I don't hold nothing against him personal. When it comes to the dogs, he's on the square. If he can show us that we are cruel and are doing wrong by the dogs, I'll burst the pit and give away or sell my dogs, and I've got some of the finest ratters out there. Yet, I can hardly make myself believe it's cruel or wrong to kill rats."

Harry is looking at Kit with disbelief. "Kit, you must be going soft in the head. These brutes were made to fight; look at them. And when they're goin' at it, they got devil eyes and voices."

"Don't we train them to be riled up like that for the contest? When these two are in my lap, they're like my own children. Ain't ya got no feelin's?"

"Feelin's? I ain't got no feelin's as long as I git my money."

"All right," Kit replies, "I never welched on you or nobody. You want to be in the first contest of next month, I'll put you in."

"Thanks, Kit."

When night falls the next day, the local drunkards, sailors, street hooligans and uptown seekers of excitement come out in search of nightspots to satisfy their primal urges. In the alley behind Water Street, Henry Bergh and four of his agents make their way down the alley by the light of a full moon and arrive at the rear of No. 273, the infamous Sportsman's Hall. One of the agents is Andy Potter, who turns out to be the beer delivery driver who saw Kit Burns earlier in the day. He leads them to their destination.

"That's Sportsman's Hall, sir," Agent Andy points out.

Henry views the location with contempt, "Sportsmen indeed. Those folks are neither athletes nor hunters, but merely leading a so-called sporting life of drinking, gambling, whoring and other disreputable activities."

"Yes, sir," Andy answers dutifully. "That's the entrance they bring the rats in. The dogs are housed downstairs. And there's the skylight over the fighting pit. You can see it plain from the alley."

"We'll surprise Mr. Burns and his ratbaiting enthusiasts with a theatrical entrance, gentlemen." Henry turns to the agent standing to his left. "Bill, you and I will go up to the skylight. Gus and Rich, you cover the front and back doors."

"We'll have to be careful of Kit's lookouts hanging around in front," Andy answers, "They're Irish boys, and they usually conceal knives and clubs."

"The Irish are a priest-ridden and discontented race, probably responsible for three-quarters of all the cruelty to animals in this city," Henry responds.

Andy adds, "They often wear brass knuckles, sir."

"Then you be careful not to engage them," Henry advises. "Commissioner Harris tells me that while they comprise less than half the population of our city, they make up more than two-thirds of the criminals in our jails. What time is it?"

"Nine-thirty, sir."

Two police paddy wagons marked "4th Ward" turn the corner and begin traveling up the alley toward Bergh and his agents. Bergh sees them and puts up his hand to indicate they should stop. The wagons stop and half a dozen policemen emerge.

Henry turns to Agent Bill, "Go tell them to hold their positions until we are ready."

Bill runs down the alley briskly to the police.

Inside the smoke-filled back room of Sportsman's Hall, a rowdy group of yahoos and gambling men surrounds the fighting pit where a terrier will be released with wharf rats. The dog will aggressively attack the rats one by one to their bloody ends. The crowd is betting on the number of rats killed in an allotted time.

No one is aware of what is going on just outside their view, as Kit Burns is collecting cash wagers from the patrons. There's drinking and laughing and a game of dice in one corner, but the main event in the pit is about to take place. A man in a checked jacket holds a white terrier at ringside and is petting it constantly as the dog is very hyper.

One spectator calls out impatiently, "Come on, Kit! My bet's down and I'm counting on Spotty here to take all of 'em in under four minutes."

A second spectator chimes in, "You don't know Spotty. Under two minutes if he's not been fed today!" The comment is greeted with lots of laughter.

Kit Burns speaks, "All right, keep your shirts on, you mugs. Last call! All bets in! Mr. Casey, bring in the loyal opposition."

From the side enters Mr. Casey, holding a burlap sack with his arm outstretched. Inside the sack, small animals are thrashing about. Now the crowd gets excited with men whistling and whooping in anticipation. He approaches the side of the pit opposite where the man holding his dog is standing.

Burns calls out, "Liberate them, mister."

Casey bends down and allows a dozen large rats to emerge from the sack. The rats begin running around the pit as the crowd cheers. Burns signals the man holding the dog to hold off releasing him as the dog sees the rats and gets very agitated.

As Burns is about to signal the dog's release, and the man begins to bend down toward the pit, the crowd is surprised by whistles blowing as Henry Bergh and Agent Andy swing open the skylight above them and leap down into the pit flashing their badges. Police appear with batons in hand as the doors swing open. The raid has begun in full swing.

Henry calls out in his loudest voice, "Everyone stay where you are. You're under arrest for violating the state's anticruelty law."

There is angry pandemonium as the police move in to start arresting Casey, the man who is still holding his dog and the myriad of surprised and hostile spectators.

"Officer Boseman, take Mr. Burns into custody," Henry orders.

The burly New York policeman handcuffs Kit Burns. Boseman directs his men to start taking the patrons out to the paddy wagons in cuffs. There is cursing and arguing and spitting among the angry victims of swift justice, whose ranks are used to eluding the long arm of the law. But not tonight.

The raid is a satisfying success for Henry Bergh. A little while later, as the police finish carting off more than forty-five people, Kit Burns is escorted to a paddy wagon as Henry Bergh is locking up the rear door of his Sportsman's Hall.

Burns defiantly calls out to Henry, "Mr. Bergh, for the dogs maybe I can understand your affections, but what men have sympathy for rats?"

Henry turns and walks over to Burns, meeting the man in custody almost nose to nose. "Mr. Burns, rats have more practical utility than the thief or drunkard. Take him away." Burns is led away to the paddy wagon.

The ASPCA is charged with holding all the animals from the rat and dog fight for the Court of General Sessions. A few days later, an item in the *Sun* states, "Mrs. Christopher Burns has decided to transfer her residence and the Burns family to Brooklyn, where, she intimates, she will be pleased to receive a call from Mr. Bergh, providing that humane gentleman will have the kindness to bring his coffin with him." The threat is ironic inasmuch as before Kit Burns could appear in court, he is stricken with diphtheria and dies at age forty-four.

Following Burns's demise, Sportsman's Hall is leased to a Methodist minister for prayer meetings and, despite the closing of Kit Burns's fighting ring, animal fighting remains a persistent and lucrative business, though perhaps less frequently, cropping up in livery stables and warehouses or wherever the inhumane entrepreneurs can surreptitiously locate them and evade the authorities.

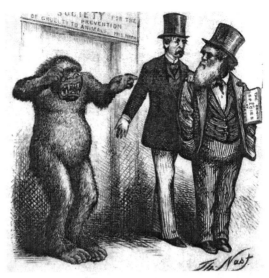

Illus. 14 - Thomas Nast caricatures "Mr. Bergh to the Rescue"
The Defrauded Gorilla: That *Man* wants to claim my pedigree.
He says he is one of my Descendants.
Mr. Bergh: Now, Mr. Darwin, how could you insult him so?

THE FRIEND OF THE BRUTES.

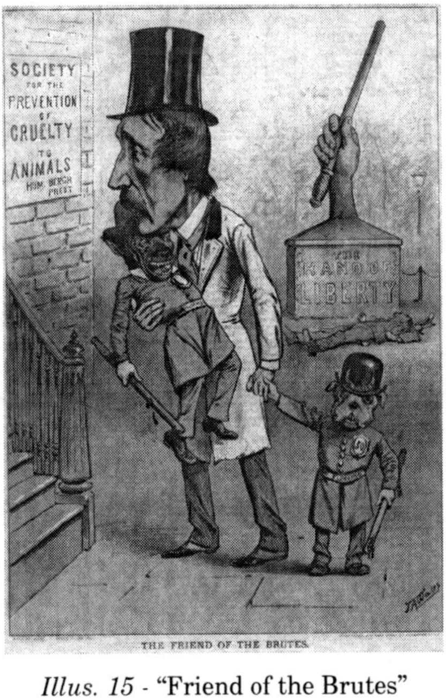

Illus. 15 - "Friend of the Brutes"

Illus. 16 - Stray dogs are drowned in the East River.

Illus. 17 - *Dog Fighting* at Sportsmen's Hall

Illus. 18 - Rat Baiting at Sportsmen's Hall

Illus. 19 - The arrest of Kit Burns

CHAPTER 7

Henry Bergh and Elbridge Gerry are men in their fifties to whom life is still a sophisticated and complex balancing act. Married life has many benefits, but for men over fifty, the reality of waning sex lives at home poses challenges for respectable men. They know the urge to seek sensual companionship would be morally wrong, but at the same time many of their peers were roundly enjoying extramarital sex in obscure nightclubs, brothels and apartments. When friends and acquaintances bragged of such liaisons, only the most prudish of men would not want to vicariously congratulate the cheaters and seek out the same enjoyment. Temptation is the universal test that all civilized men endure from ancient times to now, and New York City is rife with opportunities in the glorious nineteenth century.

Henry and Elbridge often walk the streets of New York to discuss strategy, clear their heads from the oppression of their work responsibilities and observe the street life in the city, which is dotted with restaurants and pubs, galleries and music halls and a lively population of street people. When the sun goes down, the city turns into a melange of social activities, spanning a spectrum only few know completely. One of the more curious amusements for mature men to attend is being advertised on a colorful poster that a worker is just finishing pasting up, and Henry and his attorney stop to read it. It is for a private exhibition called *Tableaux Vivant*. This one is entitled "Walhalla" and describes a series of scantily clad artist models posing in still-life scenes including *Venus Rising from the Sea* and *Lady Godiva, or Peeping Tom of Coventry*.

The history of these exhibitions dates back to a little-known Englishman named Frimbley, who used to dress himself neatly in skintight, cotton clothes, which he then doused all over with flour. From the audience, he looked very much like a plaster-of-paris statue. Frimbley would throw himself into all sorts of shapes and attitudes and pose in well-chosen, exaggerated positions that recollected a favorite classical painting or statue, such as *Ajax Defying the Lightning, The Dying Gladiator* and two or three others, equally classic and effective. These representations were very popular all over England and were really well worth seeing, for Frimbley was a good artist and studied his attitudes carefully. He had been originally a dancing and fencing master, comic pantomimist and stage dancer and might have made a fortune by his "living statues," but he was strongly given to drink. It was rumored that he had died miserably, in some obscure place, without friends or money to bury him. Now and then, imitators of Frimbley had appeared, singly or in groups, but they never made any sensation, simply because they were not artists and their exhibitions were merely ama-teurish imitations.

Shortly after the Civil War ended, an Englishman named Robert H. Collyer, formerly known as a traveling animal magnetizer, returned to New York from a visit to his native land advertising what he called a troupe of "model artists." Up to this time, these exhibitions had been composed exclusively of men, and despite the men posing practically naked, there was no objection from the keepers of public morality because the scenes portrayed classical art. However, the moment women made their appearance in the exhibitions, an outcry of outraged public decency rose on all sides. Despite such objections, the shows were not driven underground and freely advertised in public. The authorities, being principally male, overlooked this marginal vice, deeming it harmless.

Collyer was familiar with the science of manipulating the public and proceeded very adroitly. At first, vague and mysterious paragraphs appeared in respectable papers whenever possible to the effect that "the celebrated Dr. Collyer" had organized in Rome or London a company of models, both men and women, who stand or sit for the painters of the academies and who are of course selected expressly on account of their symmetry and beauty of form, some for voluptuousness, some for strength, some for grace and delicacy and other such claims. The announcements promised they would give representations of scriptural and classic pictures, being draped and grouped in strict accordance with the works of the great masters. When the exhibition opened, however, it was found that the living statuary portraying classical art was only a part of the entertainments. The rest of the exhibition comprised a variety of tableaus portraying scenes of men and woman enjoying the pleasures of wine, song and salaciousness in both classical and contemporary settings, as well as dances in which the scantily clad models pranced about the stage with the accompaniment of a single harp or violin, groping each other in titillating choreography that had only one purpose.

To decent people, these exhibitions were neither immodest nor exciting, simply obscene and disgusting. The female models were far from being models from the European academies, but more often had stepped from the brothel to the public stage or were young women from the country, destitute of home, friends and work and compelled to adopt this profession for the sole purpose of avoiding destitution. Collyer's exhibitions were constantly crowded at first, and within a short time, other "model artist" exhibitions were cropping up all over town, populated with abandoned women of the lowest strata who managed to earn a bare subsistence, unable to market themselves in any other way. In many of the establishments where these events took place, men and women sometimes performed the dances in a state of complete nudity. They employed every device to increase the "richness" of these onstage orgies and appeal to the male patrons' most prurient interests. A complaint to the authorities the previous October resulted in the police arriving and finding a squad of naked Olympians at a converted warehouse on Twenty-first Street, wherein Venus was trundled off to New York's Hall of Justice and the municipal prison known as the Tombs in a wheelbarrow, minus her chemise, and Bacchus had a narrow escape through a back window, leaving his trousers behind, while the Three Graces, as naked as they were born, made an unsuccessful attempt to ungracefully scramble out a back basement window.

Nothing very serious ever came of the charges, the model artist exhibitions, being numerous and popular as ever, continued with casual immunity from municipal inspection or opposition. The audiences of worn-out rakes and sensualists, ambitious young libertines and hypocritical old lechers who sneak into these exhibitions to gloat over the salacious gesticulations of the poor models continued to attend to satiate their sexual appetites.

"What do you think, Henry?" Elbridge asks as Henry stares, fixated on the illustrated poster's colorful images of ethereal ladies with hour-glass figures and heaving bosoms. The poster beckons patrons to enter the stable next door.

"I think it's fair to say that this exhibition is worthy of our investigation."

"Oh, yes?" Elbridge responds.

Henry points to the lower right side of the imagery. In the background, behind a strawberry blonde wearing a tight bustier and a flowing chiffon boa, is pictured a divan with a King Charles Cavalier dog seated on a red cushion. "If that animal is featured in the program, it's our duty to ensure its care." Henry winks at Elbridge and proceeds to the entrance, gesturing for him to follow.

The two men enter a dirty stable thatched with straw and reeking knee-deep in filth and manure. Beside the main entrances for the horses to stagger through at night is a small door opening upon a dark passage, at the end of which they stumble up a narrow staircase and find themselves in a dimly lighted room, the famous "Walhalla," residence of gods and goddesses and evidently directly over the stable. The front is occupied by a rough counter furnished with bottles of variously colored raw whiskey, which passes under the various names of brandy, gin, Jamaica or cherry bounce, according to the taste of the customer. A few fetid camphene lamps, hung at dreary intervals along the walls, exhale a gentle lamp-black shower upon the air. The aroma mingling with odors from the stable and the smoke of American cigars is certainly unpleasant. The floor is slippery with mud and tobacco juice. A green rag rug runs across the lower end of the room, and at one corner sit two men, one scraping a villainous fiddle and the other punishing a rheumatic piano. The music changes to a slow and plaintive air, a little bell jingles and up goes the rag curtain at the end of the room.

Henry and Elbridge pay their admission to an old man and find seats on rickety wooden folding chairs. Referring to their program, they ascertain that the first tableau is *Susannah in the Bath*. The same brawny female who is also listed as Venus, Psyche and the Greek Slave is now seated as Susannah in her bath, with her face and frontage to the audience. A light gauze drapery is held in her right hand and falls in a kind of demi-curtain before her knees, otherwise she is nude. Behind her are the "elders," stooping and leaning over each other, trying to get a good view. Susannah, seated upon the "revolving pedestal of Canova," commences her circumgyrations, and when she has got nearly once round, one of the elders begins speaking to his neighbor in his excitement, as he dropped his plug of tobacco on the ground, which startles the fair Susannah, who raises her hand, still holding the little curtain, to her head. The consequence brings delight to the audience. And in this condition she completes her revolution before the audience, who roundly yell and catcall with delight as the curtain goes down, continuing their furious applause until the very old horses in the stable below wake up and whinny their response. Overcome by these unexpected demonstrations of popularity, the obliging artiste comes out again and goes through the same performance again, without stopping to take breath. After the third performance of the same begins to play out once again, Henry and Elbridge had had enough and exit, heading for home with good examples of their manhood waiting for their spouses.

Henry Bergh's interest in the female of the species was usually restricted to that of a voyeur rather than a philanderer. His notoriety as the head of a high-profile New York institution was a fact of life that he needed to protect from scandal or gossip. The ASPCA was a protector of public morals regarding animal welfare, but the same respectable standards needed to apply across all social conduct. Henry was, on one hand, obsessed with setting an example, but on the other hand, conflicted with his primal need to observe and analyze women in all walks of life, especially those populating the lower classes with whom he was least familiar personally, and document their activities for his writings. At a cotillion, he was the dutiful husband and perfect gentleman who could innocently flirt and flatter the wives and daughters in a fatherly way. However, when his relentless curiosity and penchant for observing the entire spectrum of humankind would take over, after work he would slip away and walk to parts of the city populated by sailors and streetwalkers, gamblers and fancy men, pickpockets and burglars. On such trips, he would leave behind his customary top hat, remove the gold badge from his lapel and wear a brown derby with a knit muffler if the weather was cool. He also replaced his pince-nez reading glasses with horn-rimmed glasses, so he was less likely to be recognized.

On a blustery evening in March, Henry is once again the last one out of the office. After locking up, he walks south on Broadway toward downtown, passing fashionable shops illuminated with bright gaslight fixtures and well-dressed pedestrians rushing to get home or rendezvous for dinner at a fine restaurant with a spouse or lover. Crossing Crosby Street, the neighborhood starts to change. The streets are darker and less populated. The elegant storefronts turn to pubs and oyster cellars, with their bright lamps casting broad gleams of red light across the street. At one entrance is a party of rowdy and half-drunken young men on their way to the theater, the gambling house, the bowling saloon or the brothel, while one man is vomiting on the other stairway, having already swilled his fill of oysters and bad brandy. Passing them, Henry can smell their reeking mouths and their atrocious cigars, which the barkeeper recommended as "full-flavored." Close at their heels follows the bill-sticker with his posters over one arm and his paste bucket hanging on the other. He surveys the fresh bills put up by others and carefully and neatly plasters over them with his own.

Henry stops to observe two ladies across the street who have caught his attention. Their complexions are pure white and red, and their dresses are of the most expensive material. Diamonds and bracelets flash from their half-naked voluptuous bosoms and bare arms, and scarlet India shawls hang carelessly from their bare shoulders, almost trailing on the walk. Their bright eyes look invitingly at every passerby. But for their large feet and vulgar hands, they would be taken for upper-class ladies. Henry knows better. They walk with a free and sweeping gait and shuffle their feet on the flagstones with a noise that sets Henry's teeth sharply on edge.

The ladies approach a young man who stops and stares wistfully at them, hesitates, then goes on, but he slows and then retraces his steps and walks cautiously down the side street. The two "fishers of men," seeing that there is some game afoot, have now separated. The younger and better-looking one keeps walking on the main street, while her companion, casting a leering glance at the young man and scraping her feet, tosses her head and follows the young man down the side street, but on the other side. The victim knows not exactly what to make of it, wonders if he is mistaken, but makes up his mind that it is time for his first essay in vice. The painted demon who has lured him on looks hard at him, and Henry can hear her exclaim familiarly, "How do you do, my dear? Come, won't you go home with me?" The young man is pleased. He crosses the street to the one who has lured him.

"From this moment his doom is sealed," Henry thinks. "Need I follow him to the filthy street, the squalid chamber where the prostitute performs her trade and ends by robbing her clients with a panel thief, who is her compatriot hiding behind a wall panel? Not tonight."

Despite the rise of the Temperance Movement in the years before the Civil War and the formation of the New York Society for the Suppression of Vice in 1873, brothels are still found in every neighborhood in the city. Their existence is well-disguised over dry goods stores, milliners and tobacco shops, next to ice cream parlors and bowling saloons and even down the street from churches. Their stealthy existence is known to the local men who patronize them and to the sailors, greenhorns and other travelers entering the city in search of excitement and stimulation. Many are run-down hovels where sex is offered along with disease and robberies, and others are finely appointed dwellings, richly carpeted and furnished, gaslit with beautiful chandeliers and offering entertainment of piano music and bar service.

While Mr. Gerry is taking advantage of his prosperity and occasional free time with a *joie de vivre* that most men only fantasize about, Mr. Bergh is riddled with self-doubt about his male persona that he thinks is being ravaged by various new wrinkles and a receding hairline with each passing day.

Henry's early experience with the beautiful Hannah of the Bowery has colored his opinion of ladies of the evening, seeing them as sensuous and elusive curiosities. When his beloved Hannah disappeared, Henry never wanted to feel that heartache again, and so he began a journey that takes him to many brothels and dens of iniquity, not to sleep with its inhabitants, but searching to discover what makes the female of the species tick. Such quest would haunt him for the rest of his life.

The time spent together with the working women that society calls "fallen women" was more of an interview than a liaison. The ladies were more than happy to get paid to talk and drink with this tall, well-mannered stranger. Henry considered the experiences research, as he would make notes afterward that he would use to create characters and dialogue in his plays.

Henry particularly enjoyed the company of the young, fresh prostitutes who had the bloom of womanly innocence still lingering here and there on their powdered cheeks, pretending that the outward form could hide the inner turmoil and depravity they so skillfully conceal. It's the young ones that are in that transitional period between the purity and peace of virtue and the swinish hell of filth and abomination into which too many of them were doomed to plunge and wallow until an early death by disease, violence or simply natural causes.

As Henry spends time with more and more of these women, he sees them not as the demons society casts them but rather as tragic victims of neglect, betrayed by the men their young hearts loved and then abandoned by the world that should have protected them. The result of this double lesson has convinced them that the gratification of the present moment is the only real and good thing in life and that all the talk about virtue and reputation and crime and punishment is a tiresome waste of their time.

But there is the occasional whore with a saucy eye and scarlet petticoat who imparts some wisdom to Henry. One evening he arrives at Madam Claudia's on Great Jones Street, which turns out to be the most expensive and aristocratic house of vice Henry has every visited. Likely in her sixth decade, Madam Claudia is an elegant, raven-haired former beauty who was either Jewish or Italian, depending on what night of the week you asked her. Her clothing is elegant but unadorned, in contrast to her girls, who sit around on luxurious sofas and divans wearing paste diamonds and rubies in a large, warm parlor that has hallways leading to a half dozen private rooms.

"Madam Claudia," Henry greets her, "it's a pleasure to see you again," he bows slightly and removes his hat.

"Henry, you are looking more handsome every day," she oozes.

"Have you any new girls tonight? It's been more than two months since I was last here."

"I think you'll be very pleased to meet Cynthia, just arrived from Boston." She turns and leads Henry to an attractive blonde in a bustier seated by an oil lamp, reading a book. "My dear, this is Henry."

The girl rises and is quite tall, which impresses Henry who stands six foot two. She extends her hand.

He takes it gently as he bows respectfully. The two retire to a well-appointed private chamber furnished with a four-poster bed. Henry sits in an easy chair, and the girl begins to disrobe.

"That won't be necessary. I'm not here for sex," Henry tells her matter-of-factly, as he takes out a small notebook and pencil. "I just want to talk."

"Talk? About what?" she inquires of the unusual request.

"You. Your life. Your thoughts. You needn't reveal anything you're not comfortable with. I am a writer and therefore a student of human nature. My stories require characters that speak truthfully. Call our conversation research, if you like."

Sitting on the edge of the bed, she doesn't bother to rebutton her bustier, but suddenly smiles wryly. "Can you still do it?"

He looks up, "Yes. Not for as long as I used to be able to as a younger man, but it still works. Do you mind if I ask you some questions?"

"If that's your pleasure, go right ahead," she responds as she hitches herself upon the bed and makes herself comfortable.

"What was growing up for you like?"

She purses her mouth for a moment, thinking before she answers. "The first thing I can remember is being cold and hungry and wearing rags for clothes. My parents sent me out on rainy mornings into the street to sweep the crossing and beg for pennies."

"How did that work?"

"I would take my broom and walk over to Hanover and Charter Streets looking for well-dressed pedestrians who would throw me a few coins for sweeping away the mud and manure in their way. I was only a wee child, and they would pity me."

"Who did you live with?"

"I lived with my mother and father and two older brothers."

"Where?"

"In a cellar room down an alley in the north end near the docks."

"What was the room like?"

"There was almost no daylight coming in from one little window up high where my father had put rags to close a hole in the glass. The floors were loose boards where black mud and slime would ooze up through the cracks when it rained. The fireplace didn't work, and the room would pretty much fill up with smoke all winter. The damp used to come out on the walls and stand there in big gummy drops. There was a little closet in one corner of the room and a pine table against the wall with three or four wooden chairs. Two of them broke and became just stools. And a pile of shavings and rubbish by the door. I remember it well because it was the only home for my childhood. I knew no other place or shelter. It's where we slept, ate, cooked, washed and ironed; we did everything in this one dreadful room."

"What were your parents like?"

"They were mostly kind to me and each other. They never beat me when I had been unlucky in my day's work. When my mother would see me come home with my little frozen fingers almost empty, crying and dragging my old broom, she would comfort me, showing affection. Much more so than anyone has shown for me later, I can tell you that."

"What else do you remember about your parents?"

"They both liked to drink whiskey whenever they got a chance. I imbibed in it at an early age, and even though I found it terrible in smell and taste, after I drank it I felt like another being. I was beautiful and wore fine clothes and had on pretty shoes and stockings, like the fine little girls I saw walking with their mamas on the promenade."

"So drink was transformative?"

"Excuse me?"

"It made you feel better about your life."

"Oh, yes. Most times I pined and longed for a life I never knew with a vague and fierce feeling of despair and revenge that filled my little heart almost to bursting. But when I had a lucky day, my father used to give me a drink of raw whiskey out of his bottle and, oh, I felt glorious and forgave and loved everybody! I tell you, drunkenness is the only thing left to a poor woman in this world."

"When did you leave home?"

"When I got to be about twelve or thirteen, they wanted me to stop street-sweeping and take to thieving. But I hadn't been on the street crossing four or five years for nothing, and I had formed designs of a different character."

"What do you mean?"

"In a word, I was ambitious. When I saw I was growing into a woman and the handsome young clerks and rich old lechers at the crossings on their way to work were beginning to notice me, I decided to make my own way through the world."

"How?"

"Well, first I had secreted away some money that I used to buy some secondhand clothes that looked better than what I had and wore them on just certain days. Around that same time, I had formed a sort of acquaintance with a handsome, beautifully dressed lady who used to occasionally stop and give me a sixpence and talk to me. She always wore brightly colored dresses and longer feathers than the other ladies. She looked so fine with cheeks that were so red and teeth that were so white that I supposed she was the mayor's wife or perhaps a queen come over on a visit. One day, she gave me a sixpence and as I took it from her hand, she took mine and asked if I wanted to come work for her. She treated me honorably and when I became her assistant, she told me my duties and I was happy to work for her. I spent time with old men of means, most who were blind with debauchery and palsied with age. After I grew, that game couldn't be carried on any longer and I passed for a young widow for younger sparks to squander their money on me. I've fleeced a pretty good number of such villains and mean to do so to a great many more," she laughs sardonically.

"And what is your life like today?" Henry asks her as he continues to make notes.

"When I compare the squalid, loathsome, suffocating home of my childhood to my life today, I ought to be pretty well-satisfied with what I have today. I live freely and generously. I dress like a princess. I drink, eat and sleep like a king's mistress. And I care for nobody on earth."

"Aren't you ever lonely?"

"Sometimes, to be sure, I feel a kind of heartsickness when I am alone or when it is a rainy, dismal day that reminds me of when I used to stand barefooted and shivering on the crossing begging for pennies. At such times something seems to whisper to me that I am a horrible creature. But that spell of gloom doesn't stay with me very long. A good stiff glass of brandy and water sets me all right again, and I don't care what society thinks of me, nor anything else."

Henry looks up at her and smiles sympathetically, if not a bit awkwardly.

"You don't have to feel sorry for me, mister. I know I am a demon, a she-devil, as are all women who have lost their virtue, and I mean to make the most of it."

"One more question. As far as love-making abilities, do you prefer to be with a rich man or a poor man?"

She responds, "Frankly, I prefer the colored man's technique."

CHAPTER 8

Henry Bergh enters the Court of Special Sessions with Elbridge Gerry. *The People vs. Captain Nehemiah Calhoun and the Newfoundland Shipping Company* is on the docket this morning, and the two men, representing the ASPCA, are there to prosecute the case. Henry sits in the front row of the gallery, and Gerry goes directly to the front of the room to the district attorney, who is seated at the prosecution's table. Gerry pulls out the chair and sits next to him, and they proceed to speak quietly.

Captain Calhoun and his lawyer, Martin Stone, enter and are directed by the clerk to be seated at the defendant's table. The judge enters the courtroom and the clerk calls out, "Hear ye, hear ye, all rise, this court is now in session, the honorable Judge Frederick Adams presiding. Be seated."

Judge Adams begins, "I've read the complaint by the Society for the Prevention of Cruelty to Animals against Captain Nehemiah Calhoun, and it is my understanding that the conditions endured by live turtles in shipment is the subject of this proceeding."

Mr. Gerry responds, "Yes, your honor. I am Elbridge Gerry, representing the Society."

"Your society has been in this court before on such matters, has it not?"

Gerry replies, "Not exactly, your honor. The Society has prosecuted several cases involving the mistreatment of horses, cattle and dogs in public settings. This case involves the manner in which live animals transported on the high seas were treated below deck at port."

"Proceed," the judge directs.

"Yes, your honor. Captain Nehemiah Calhoun and his crew were taken into custody and charged with cruelty to eighty-six sea turtles transported from Newfoundland in March after Mr. Henry Bergh, the president of the Society for the Prevention of Cruelty to Animals, became aware of the shipment and obtained a search warrant from Magistrate Walters to board the ship at port and inspect the conditions. He is here to testify today.

"You may call your witness."

"I call to the stand Henry Bergh."

Henry rises, crosses to the witness stand, is sworn in and takes a seat.

Mr. Gerry begins, "Now, Mr. Bergh, could you tell the court what you observed on March 22nd of this year?"

"Yes. I boarded the schooner *Active* at approximately noon, accompanied by twelve of my SPCA agents in uniform, for the purposes of inspecting the conditions under which we learned that sea turtles had been shipped a great distance."

"Were you able to do so?"

"Yes."

"And what did you find?" Mr. Gerry inquires.

"We were escorted below deck where I observed that the entire ship's hold was filled with live sea turtles. We eventually counted eighty-six of them."

"And in what state did you find the turtles?"

"The poor creatures were all on their backs without food or water present and with their fins pierced and bound and often bloodied at the wound sites. Having the creatures turned over on their backs is an uncomfortable and unnatural position for a turtle to be experiencing."

"And how do you know that it is uncomfortable and unnatural?" Mr. Gerry asks.

"Common sense dictates that it is so, and we also consulted with the notable naturalist and professor of zoology at Harvard University, Louis Agassiz, who was kind enough to publish his opinions in this letter, from which *The New York Times* quoted extensively."

Mr. Gerry interrupts, "Your honor, we wish to enter such letter as Exhibit A," as he takes the letter from his witness and hands it to the judge. Continuing, "And what did you do upon observing this scene?"

"I instructed my men to cut the ropes that bound the creatures together and prevented them from moving and right them and then placed Captain Calhoun and his crew under arrest."

"Could you describe the physical condition of the turtles that you observed?"

"They were clearly malnourished and dehydrated. Their eyes were glassy and heads leaning all the way back as if their spirits had been broken. It was a shocking and disheartening scene. I doubt if the creatures would have lived another day or two in such circumstances."

"Was there any conversation between you and the defendant at that time?"

"Yes, there was. When I asked the captain what manner of man could do this to living creatures, he responded that the shipper was responsible for their condition, not him."

"No further questions."

The judge turns to the defendant's table and asks, "Is the defendant represented by counsel?"

The defense attorney rises. "He is, your honor. I am Martin Stone."

"You may cross-examine the witness."

"Thank you, your honor. Now Mr. Bergh, you have become somewhat of a celebrity since you began your Society. We see stories about you in the newspapers and cartoons memorializing your activities and expertise on behalf of the animals."

Bergh quips, "I'm glad you're here to see me in person, so you'll know I don't look like those cartoons," which prompts some laughter among the spectators.

Stone continues, "Yes, but let me ask you if I may, sir, are you familiar with the expression, 'a little knowledge is a dangerous thing?'"

Henry answers him simply, "Yes."

"Would you tell the court what you think that means."

"Well, I suppose it means a person who operates on a basis of limited knowledge or experience could cause considerable harm."

Satisfied, attorney Stone continues, "I couldn't have put it more concisely myself. So, obviously, this expression would not apply to you because you are a trained expert on the subject of animals."

Henry interjects, "No, I never said that, but I don't believe a trained expert is required to discern whether animals are being abused."

"I see." Stone turns toward the back of the courtroom. "Could you bring in the exhibit, please." The rear doors of the courtroom open and two men carry in a wooden box, walk up the aisle and place it on the floor next to the defense table. They lift a large turtle out of the box and place the large creature on the defense table.

"Now then, Mr. Bergh, could you tell me what this creature is?"

"A turtle."

"Not exactly, Mr. Bergh. It's a terrapin actually, that is to say, a sea turtle. Would you mind telling the court precisely what kind of sea turtle it is?"

"I don't know," Henry answers matter-of-factly.

The attorney responds dripping with sarcasm, "I am surprised that the president of the Society for the Prevention of Cruelty to Animals doesn't know his turtles."

Mr. Gerry stands, "Objection, your honor. Mr. Bergh's knowledge of the genus of sea turtles is immaterial and irrelevant to this case."

"Your honor, the defense is attempting to reach a point."

"Proceed," the judge allows.

"Now, Mr. Bergh, I believe you consider it cruel and unnatural for turtles to be kept on their backs." He gestures to the two men standing by the turtle. They turn the turtle over on its back, "In this manner."

Henry is not amused. "Correct."

"Why do you feel so strongly about it, Mr. Bergh? Do you think it hurts the turtle?"

"Of course. Forced to lie in an unnatural position for hours on end is both physically and mentally cruel."

"But you just testified that you are not an expert on animals. And yet you profess to be competent to pass judgment on whether this animal is suffering or not. You know, of course, that turtles are normally shipped in this manner, that is, on their backs."

"That is only because they are unable to escape their captors while they are in that position."

"Well, not exactly, Mr. Bergh. The reason they are shipped on their backs is that when they are transported in their so-called natural position, they will often chafe themselves so badly they must be destroyed."

Mr. Gerry stands, "I object, your honor, the statement is made without any proof or foundation."

Mr. Stone rebuts, "But your honor, we do have proof." The attorney picks up papers from the defendant's table. "I have here affidavits from a renowned zoologist and from several shipping firms affirming that what I have just stated is the truth. Would you care to see them before I offer them into evidence, Mr. Bergh?"

"No."

Mr. Stone hands the papers to the judge. "No further questions for this witness."

The judge looks to Henry, "You may step down, Mr. Bergh."

The prosecution proceeded to call as witnesses the president of the New York Health Board and an editor of *The Sanitarian*, who both testified that the treatment of the turtles in question not only caused them pain and suffering but also vitiated the flesh of the animals as food for human consumption, possibly leading to "strange and incurable diseases" if consumed by innocent gourmands.

Mr. Gerry rested the prosecution's case with confidence that he had proven what he had set out to prove. But, the captain's attorney, Mr. Stone, would mount a vigorous defense. He calls Captain Calhoun to the stand, who defends himself as an innocent middleman who was merely carrying out his duties. On cross-examination, Mr. Gerry is unable to move the captain on humane grounds from his defense. He is a hired hand, no more no less.

The head of the shipping company testifies that shipping the turtles in any other manner would render them unsuitable for sale and destroy the market for this product. Mr. Gerry grills the shipper on cross-examination about the moral ethics of profiteering on the suffering of animals, but the man is unmoved and unapologetic.

When the defense calls a Baptist minister to testify about the turtles he keeps in his home, Bergh and Gerry feel their case is strong and the defense is grasping at straws. The pious witness insists that he had experimented with two turtles in his backyard and that the one tied on his back felt as comfortable as the one that was free to roam around. Henry could only roll his eyes in disbelief and disgust.

After a day of testimony, the judge recesses to consider his ruling.

That evening, Henry and his lawyer dine at a small cafe on Chambers Street near the courthouse. As

Elbridge Gerry eats soup, Henry is leafing through a newspaper.

"Here it is. *The Brooklyn Times* is with us. They called Captain Calhoun, 'the cruelest captain on the high seas.' Calhoun is quoted, 'Mr. Bergh is a monomaniac on the subject. I believe his society ought to be supported, but he carries his views to extremes. If Bergh carries out his theories about what is cruel to turtles, will he next take up the cause of clams and oysters and ruin the entire seafood trade?'"

Gerry laughs. "They are afraid of us, Henry. The cost of shipping turtles our way would likely stop the trade. Why else would they call a Baptist minister with only anecdotal backyard observations as an expert witness? I mean, honestly, is this judge going to give weight to such testimony?"

The next morning, the two men return to the courthouse as Judge Adams is ready to announce his ruling. He gavels the room to silence. Bergh and Gerry anxiously await the decision.

The judge speaks. "This court has heard all the testimony in this matter. The Society has indeed raised some relevant questions as to the manner in which the defendant transports live turtles. This must be weighed in context to the current accepted practices in an industry that employs thousands of family men. Because the term 'cruelty' is a subjective one, this court finds that the turtles in question experienced nothing beyond the necessary cruelty that frequently, if not regrettably has to be used in cases of animals killed for food. Secondly, I don't believe that sea turtles are classified as animals within the language of the statute, which addresses the treatment of domestic and work animals, and therefore are not protected under the statute. Therefore, I am dismissing the complaint. Good day, gentlemen."

The judge hits his gavel, as Henry Bergh holds back his displeasure.

Riding back home from the courthouse in Henry's coach, Elbridge is attempting to appease his friend and client about today's decision.

"If we take a strategy that focuses on just the most winnable cases, then we create an atmosphere to widen that circle of case law a little at a time," Elbridge assures.

Henry in inconsolable. "'Necessary cruelty?' The courts are amoral."

"The courts are men, Henry. The judge is a man who has a family to support. He sees fishery workers as having the same goals."

"Yes, I know. But I cannot accept the legal concept of necessary cruelty."

"Look at the horse that pulls us. Are we cruel to him forcing him to work for us?"

"Not at all," Henry answers. "He is fed and groomed and kept sheltered."

"Is he happy? Do we know that for sure?"

The coach stops in front of Henry's townhouse. Henry steps out and turns back to Gerry inside. "Horses are not men, but they deserve to be treated with the same respect as men. And the same is true for turtles and all the rest of the animal kingdom."

"Goodnight, Henry," Elbridge replies.

Bergh closes the coach door and walks to the front door of his home. When he enters, removing his overcoat, he is greeted by an agitated servant. "Mr. Bergh! The missus was taken ill this afternoon. They took her to the infirmary."

"Which one?" Henry asks.

"St. Vincent's."

Henry hastily puts his overcoat back on and leaves. St. Vincent's is not far from the Bergh's townhouse on Fifth Avenue and Twenty-fourth Street. Since Henry had dismissed his coach to take Mr. Gerry home, he walks.

Henry arrives at Matilda's room, where she is alone, awake in bed, looking forlornly out the window. Henry approaches her lovingly.

"How did the turtles fare?" she asks her husband.

"We lost the battle, but we haven't lost the war."

"I'm sorry, Henry."

"The doctor says you need to rest. You'll come home soon."

Henry rests his head on Matilda's shoulder. He spends the night sleeping in a chair by his wife's bed. The next morning, Henry must leave and attend to business but promises to return before sundown.

Walking out of the hospital and down the block, Henry passes a building being constructed. Workers are lifting up large buckets from the ground to a third story with a wooden cantilevered winch and pulley. He stops to observe it with great interest. The men pulling on the rope can lift a heavy container that is certainly twice their combined weight. Always thinking about how to help animals, this scene inspires him to think about the effort it entails to move a downed horse. "Why can't we use such a device to move a horse in distress?" he thinks.

Back in his office, Henry is at his desk drawing on a large sketchpad. He refers to a book that has schematic drawings of winch and pulley devices. He is determined to make an emergency lift for horses and mount it on a wagon. His next appointment is with a craftsman who can build such a device.

Some time later, Henry Bergh and a man in blacksmith garb are inspecting with curiosity and pride a long, white wagon that has a wooden armature device. The blacksmith demonstrates to Bergh how the armature swings out from the wagon and allows the user to lower a leather harness at the end of a rope using a winch. Henry signals his approval.

The horse ambulance is an immediate success. Only a day after the vehicle is put in service and parked in front of Henry's office on Fifth Avenue, down on Mulberry Street a horse is reportedly lying in the street unable to get up. A small crowd has gathered around it, and one observer had the presence of mind to run on foot to the SPCA building and report the incident.

Only minutes later, the clanging of a bell is followed by the arrival of a white wagon pulled by two horses. On the side of the wagon is painted "A.S.P.C.A. Emergency Rescue." Four men get out of the vehicle and place the armature and winch over the horse and lower the harness to the horse. They move the horse about until they manage to secure the harness under and around the horse. Then they crank the winch until the horse is elevated to the wagon level, at which time the armature is swung around, loading the horse into the back of the wagon. The amazed spectators begin to applaud.

Thus began a campaign to actively help the horses of New York City, an urban center bustling with thousands of horse-drawn vehicles ambling up and down the streets and avenues. Because many times there was no available water for the horses to drink, even in hot weather, Henry hired masonry workers to build horse-watering stations all over the city. The first one was near Union Square. As soon as the workers finished building it and it was ready to function, Henry personally traveled down to Union Square and begin filling it with water from a water truck marked "A.S.P.C.A." Reporters from the *Sun, Times* and *Observer* were there to record Henry's personal appearance, of course. A still photographer sets up his camera and tripod, and Henry poses for a photograph with a horse in front of the fountain, but the noise of the flash powder that pops as the picture is taken surprises the horse who jolts a bit. Henry strokes the horse's mane a couple times to calm down the beast, but quickly hands the creature over to a handler more familiar with the horse.

The city was rife with problems associated with animals that now all fall on the shoulders of Henry Bergh's SPCA to address, even when other city agencies are charged with such duties. The Board of Health is charged with being vigilant in the area of food and dairy animals, because food-borne illnesses are a constant and virulent problem to the human population. But the board's resources and manpower are limited. One of the biggest vectors of sickness is what became known as swill-milk. The dairies would feed the dairy cattle unboiled swill that would transmit all sorts of germs into the milk supply. Sick and dying infants and children were of great concern to the Board of Health, as grieving mothers were a particularly powerful symbol of their failure to protect the public.

For Henry Bergh, the swill-milk problem is a two-fold issue of human health and animal protection, as the dairies were often neglectful in caring for their milking cows. ASPCA agents inspected many of the dairies and found one with particularly egregious conditions by the Williamsburg Docks. Henry decides to raid the facility and obtains a search warrant.

Just before nine A.M. on a cool Friday morning, Henry and four of his agents arrive at the scene and observe a large pile of dead cattle lying next to the Ehler's Dairy & Stables building, apparently waiting to be loaded on a barge. They approach the scene and look on with disgust as they enter the stable. Inside, Henry is holding a folded paper in his hand as he leads his men past rows of cattle being milked by milkmaids.

"The stench in here is unbearable," he says to his men. "There's no ventilation. Make a note of the acrid slop piles those cattle are feeding from; that's a sure way to produce the swill-milk that kills our children. There's no bedding for the cattle. Some are chained to upright bars where they can never lie down. This is a prison house of death."

He turns to the milkmaids. "Where's the owner of these cattle?"

The milkmaids are defiantly silent.

"This is brutal. You ought to be hung, every one of you, and these stables demolished."

Bergh and his men walk across the stable and through a broken wooden door where they encounter the owner, Mr. Ehler, a heavy-set man wearing suspenders and a visor. He is holding a sheath of papers, which he must put down when Henry serves him with the warrant and a summons. Ehler is belligerent and as he turns to walk away, Henry signals his men to stop him.

At the stable's front entrance, Bergh and his men accompany Mr. Ehler and another man in handcuffs outside.

"You can't do this!" Ehler objects loudly.

"I have a duly issued warrant, and I can and I will. Mr. Ehler, your place is in Sing Sing and Hell," Henry states calmly as Ehler arrives at the paddy wagon. "The first for violating the Milk Law and the latter for cruelty to animals."

Henry gestures to his men, who load Ehler into the paddy wagon.

News of the arrest spreads fast. At the newsroom of *The New York Tribune*, Horace Greeley, the publisher, is talking to an editor outside his office when a copy boy enters holding the paper.

"Your proof, Mr. Greeley."

"Thank you, boy."

Greeley takes it and looks at the headline: "Ehler Dairy Closed by Health Board. Owner Arrested." And the subhead: "ASPCA's Henry Bergh spearheads effort."

"Mr. Bergh has now raided four dairies accused of selling swill-milk. The Board of Health is backing him up, and I think it's time we did an extended series on the dairy industry," Greeley instructs his editor.

"I'll put O'Brien on it again," the editor tells his boss.

Back at the modest interior of the two-room ASPCA headquarters, Henry Bergh emerges from his private office with New York Governor John T. Hoffman and Agent Tommy Childs. A testament to Henry Bergh's frugality is a threadworn oriental rug in the middle of the floor.

"Governor Hoffman, thank you for supporting our efforts to reduce the swill-milk problem in our dairies. Ultimately these new laws will benefit both people and animals," Henry tells the governor as they cross the room.

"I'll make sure our friends at Tammany Hall are on board with this reform. Like you, I believe in both protecting our children and having mercy for the animals."

Henry continues, "The dairies look merciful compared to our slaughter houses. I dread to visit those butchers and have postponed going 'til it amounts to criminal neglect."

"It's not a pretty business," the governor responds.

"Three-fourths of the butchers of the city are Hebrews. Their religion obliges them to bleed to death the animals they slaughter. So they hook a chain around the hind leg of a bullock, jerk up the struggling beast head downward and cut his throat." Hoffman shakes his head. Henry goes on, "Well, their religion doesn't require them to suspend an animal by the hind leg, which frequently dislocates and lacerates the flesh. This brutal and shocking torture must be stopped."

"I agree," Hoffman responds as he looks down at a hole in the carpet and smiles. "Henry, why don't you buy yourself a new carpet and send me the bill."

"I have a better idea, Governor. You can send me the money and I'll use it to do our work for the animals." Henry smiles wryly. The two shake hands and Hoffman cheerfully exits.

Tommy Childs is one of Henry Bergh's most trusted agents. Tommy is a bright young man with ambition. He was raised in Brooklyn by his parents who owned a dry goods store on Flatbush Avenue. When not going to school, he worked the store stocking the shelves, sweeping and cleaning. Eventually his father put him to work behind the counter serving customers, as he was good-looking and well-spoken and the neighborhood thought well of him. Tommy had a penchant for reading crime novels and *The Police Gazette,* for which his mother made fun of him. For her it was low class and dwelled on the seamy side of life for which she had no tolerance. Tommy also liked hanging around the neighborhood blacksmith, especially when he was shoeing the horses. Tommy loved horses, although he had never ridden one. Tommy even volunteered to groom the horses in the neighborhood and wished his family had one of their own, but his parents were simply too busy with the store to house, feed and attend to a horse.

Tommy always knew that dry goods were not going to be his life's work. He longed to be where the action and excitement were. He finished his schooling at age seventeen and read about the newly empowered ASPCA in Manhattan and decided to take a trip across the river. Tommy sought out Henry Bergh and found him as Henry was putting the first office in order and had yet to hire a soul.

"Please, Mr. Bergh, if you hire me, I'll work twenty-five hours a day and eight days a week to protect the animals and put the cruelists in jail. I even have my own handcuffs," which he pulled out of his jacket and showed with pride. That made Henry laugh, and so he hired the enthusiastic boy on the spot, advising him, "I'm not sure cruelists is a word, son, but if it isn't, it should be."

And so in the first few years, it's Tommy Childs who becomes Henry's right-hand man for investigations and strategies, and Tommy rarely lets his boss down with innovative ways to stretch their limited resources to do the most good among a very challenging population. There is animal exploitation on every stratum of society and every geographical neighborhood. Some are worse than others, but keeping up with the reports that come in daily is daunting with only twelve agents to cover the entire city. That's why Tommy comes in early for a meeting with his boss today.

A large map of the city is spread across the conference table. Tommy is flipping through a notebook as he takes mah-jongg tiles and carefully places them on various spots on the map. Each time he places a tile, he checks off a notation in the notebook. When his boss finally arrives, he is ready. Henry Bergh is a man of punctuality and arrives at nine A.M. sharp every morning.

"Good morning, Mr. B," is Tommy's usual greeting. Henry sits down and looks over the map. The young man is eager to give his presentation.

"As you know, over the first hundred years, the city was composed of neighborhoods in lower Manhattan that became populated by people who have common backgrounds and interests." He begins to point to places on the map. "There is the Broadway-Wall Street area that represents the opulence and power of the city's 'upper ten thousand.' Then there is Chatham Street and the Bowery, composed of mostly Irish and German immigrants and their children. There's Five Points with the squalor and misery of the very poor all congregated as far as the river. And then for the past twenty or thirty years a diverse collection of others has begun to move uptown and to the other boroughs. But at the core of our jurisdiction, we have upper-class, native-born working-class and immigrant lower class living in neighborhoods that together constitute the essential structure of the city as a whole."

Henry listens attentively as he continues, "Now, with the increasing growth and complexity of the city after the War Between the States, these districts are becoming somewhat more integrated due to their close proximity. The intersection that gave the Five Points its name is only three blocks from Broadway. And there is now a massive spread of the wealthy to the north and the poor to the east of the point."

"How are we to draw any assumptions about how these various peoples treat their animals?" Henry asks.

"That's what I'm getting to," Tommy replies. He points to the mah-jongg tiles. "Each of these mah-jongg tiles represents a physical location where we have issued more than three summonses for the past year. While we can't pinpoint any one group as the worst offender, we can determine the physical locations of higher activity and try to reduce future infractions."

"How?" Henry asks.

"If we station an agent at each of these locations for, say, once or twice a week to patrol the streets in uniform and make our presence known to the general population, I believe that will discourage the most heinous conduct against animals for the fear of being taken into custody."

Henry thinks about it. "I think that is a reasonable assumption. I am concerned about diluting our central resources, though. With each agent separated from the rest, we may not be able to respond to immediate emergencies with enough manpower."

Tommy responds, "I can prepare a proposed schedule for such a plan where there is a contingency allocation of two agents at all times stationed within a half-mile of here just for such emergencies."

"Then do it," Henry instructs.

"Yes, sir," Tommy proudly replies.

Henry rises and heads for his office and adds, "Good work, my boy. Strategic thinking is the only way to attack the problem." At the door, he stops and turns, "But always remember, it's more important to change minds than laws. Our presence in the streets is an opportunity to make people think, and we need to engage them in this conversation, because the average person doesn't read the papers and the clergy has yet to convince the great unwashed to stop the murder and mayhem of one another, nonetheless the dumb animals."

"We'll do that, Mr. Bergh," Tommy responds, while taking the tiles off the map and removing the four books from each corner of the map that were used to hold it down. One of the books is a favorite of Tommy's. He glances at it and shows it to his boss. "Have you read *Moby-Dick*, Mr. Bergh?"

Henry is about to close his door when he stops abruptly and addresses the question in a tone that surprises the youth. "Mr. Melville's tribute to the unbridled hatred of our marine life? Yes, I read it. In my opinion, Captain Ahab made one mistake."

"What's that, sir?"

"The son-of-a-bitch went into the wrong line of work." He then turns and closes his door.

Illus. 20 - Henry Bergh's derrick for lifting fallen animals

Illus. 21- Horse ambulance designed by Henry Bergh

CHAPTER 9

The plight of cattle, sheep and pigs arriving for slaughter in Eastern yards is the most visible, cruel and ignored problem that Henry Bergh decides to tackle. Livestock is transported to the city by boxcar from faraway places under careless and overcrowded conditions. They arrive injured, sick, dehydrated and often dead. Yet, they are carted to slaughterhouses in any condition and processed for human consumption, often containing sickening or deadly bacteria.

Many slaughterhouses still flourish along the streets of downtown Manhattan. The Bowery reeks with the smells of adjacent establishments for entrails cleaning, hide curing, soap and fat boiling and other public nuisances. There are no laws on the books regulating this industry, and the sheer numbers of animals involved—hundreds of thousands—makes this one of Henry Bergh's most daunting challenges. Periodic raids by SPCA agents on the most egregious stockyards and butchers have been met with hostility and strong resistance to changing their methods of housing and slaughter that were created for efficiency not compassion. Even the Hebrew butchers following Jewish law called Kabbala, which is supposed to minimize suffering, inflict immense trauma on the animals before dispatching them with a *chalef*, the special knife that is used for kosher slaughter, where the blade must be at least twice as long as the neck-width of the animal to ensure that it is exposed throughout the cut and that it slices, rather than tears. It must be razor sharp and have no nicks in it whatsoever. But, the animals are almost always hoisted off the ground by one leg before slaughter to facilitate the draining of blood, and the hoisting often painfully breaks or dislocates the joint and causes the animal great pain, distress and alarm, which Henry declares an outrage to civilized men.

Henry's hard-nosed tactics of prosecuting butchers rarely result in convictions, as the courts are loath to interfere with the food-processing chain. With resources limited, humane enforcement is time-consuming. After some thought, Henry changes course and decides to address the butchers on another level—as men.

Henry Astor's Old Bull Head Tavern, headquarters of butchers, drovers and horse dealers, has moved uptown to East Twenty-fourth Street. The men have gathered after working hard all day to lift a pint of ale before going home to wife and family. They are men of all ilk, including German, Irish, Polish, Russian, Jewish, Christian, Protestant and godless men who are just trying to keep out of the poorhouse or the workhouse, for that matter. They are independent men, hard workers, and they don't take criticism of their profession lightly from wealthy do-gooders like Henry Bergh. Tonight they are passing around a pamphlet they find on the bar that Mr. Bergh composed and distributed as an olive branch, entitled "Friendly Appeal to Butchers." Bergh, unsuccessful in his attempts to change the butchers' minds about their cruel and painful practices by raiding and arresting them, hopes to sway the men with rational persuasion on a personal level.

The pamphlet begins, "Friends: As a class, we hear you spoken of as good and loyal citizens, industrious in business and civil and obliging in your dealing with fellow men. Perhaps you think that God cares only for human beings and takes no thought of other creatures whom he made. Oh friends, you are wrong! God sees! God hears! God cares! The eye that marks the sparrow's fall from Heaven is quick to note the cruel blow that man may think of little consequence. The ear that listens to young ravens when they cry, bends down to hear the low, despairing moan of the beaten and wounded beast. Remember this, each one of you, in the quiet of your happy home, with friends around you, and your wife and children at your side! Remember it, as your youngest and dearest climbs your knee and lisps out her artless evening prayer, with her lips close against your cheek. Remember it as you lie down to sleep peacefully in your bed. The solemn starlit night that brings you rest and happiness, shines down also upon the blood-stained stones of your slaughterhouses and upon the dumb, despairing sufferers there."

Sporadic titters turn into roars of laughter rolling throughout the tavern as the rough and tumble men read Bergh's appeal with derision.

"Well ain't he the diplomat?" cries one working man still wearing his blood-spattered apron. "We should send him back to Russia!" The remarks are greeted with scattered cheers.

"Let him eat turnips if he don't like our beef," says another man.

"Maybe if the man worked a day he would know what it's like to feed a family with the sweat of your brow," declares an older man with blond whiskers, downing his pint sloppily.

Tommy Childs is sitting quietly in the corner, wearing civilian clothes and listening to the adverse reaction to his boss's unsuccessful attempt to sway opinion among the slaughterhouse workers. After the men begin crumpling up and tossing the pamphlets on the floor and into spittoons, Tommy calmly rises and heads for the front door. He dreads having to report the scene to his boss the following morning.

Undaunted by his failure at friendly persuasion, Henry's steely resolve is strengthened to oppose the livestock abusers. He strategizes with his agents to map out all the hot spots and redouble his efforts to raid their premises and haul away the worst offenders to jail. As always, Henry confides in Matilda of his failure to appeal to the butchers on a humane level and his new plan for an all-out assault. She is immediately apprehensive.

"Henry, I am worried that you will incur the wrath of violent men. You must know what some of these brutes are capable of?" she warns.

"If I acquiesce to fear, I am not a man who deserves the title I hold. This is a war, my dear. A holy war that I intend to wage with all the ammunition at my disposal. When our founding father John Adams declared that we are a nation of laws, not of men, he wields a powerful sword."

"I believe Mr. Adams actually stated, 'We are a government of laws, not of men.'" She smiles wryly at him, but there is tension in her face.

"Am I not the government?" he snaps back.

"You are not the government, my dear. You are an agent of justice, but I want you to return home to me each night unharmed by the forces of ignorant men pushed to the brink. You must take care to not inflame these angry men to a breaking point. They will take retribution."

"Their wicked ways will come to an end. To look into the eyes of those tortured creatures is what I am concerned with. They need me."

"And I guess you need them," she states despondently. He sees that she is upset and moves to comfort her. "I need you, too. Don't ever forget that. I won't put myself in harm's way. I have twelve of the bravest soldiers to watch my back, and I will be home each night and every night," he reassures her.

The Davis, Atwood & Crane slaughterhouse on West Thirty-ninth Street is the target of the ASPCA's next raid. The place is a hotbed of cruelty for the hundreds of cattle and hogs it processes daily. With more than thirty butchers and two dozen assistants, it is one of the larger facilities operating in Manhattan. It comprises an entire city block and is located just one block from the Hudson River, where the loaded rail cars terminating in New Jersey meet the ferries that transport their livestock across the river to Manhattan.

The managing partner is Elmer Davis, an Oklahoma-born cowboy turned entrepreneur who moved to New York City with his first load of cattle a dozen years ago to open his own stockyard. He soon after partnered with a couple of butchers who borrowed money from their families to build a full-service stockyard and slaughter-house containing almost a thousand head, and their successful operation thrives on their quick turnaround of animals. That efficiency means creature comfort is the last consideration while the livestock is in their custody. Davis's tobacco-chewing swagger creates fear among his employees, who have seen his temper flare regularly. When the operation slows down for any reason, Davis becomes a madman, cursing and throwing whatever animal parts have fallen on the ground at the employees responsible for the snag.

Henry arrives with his men, all twelve of them, but not with the usual police paddy wagon that accompanies them on larger raids. Today he is planning to issue citations and make a record of the facility's conditions. He is dressed in his usual long coat and stovepipe hat, sports his gold badge on his lapel and holds a handful of folded paper citations that have already been filled out that he is ready to issue. The posse spreads out and enters the yards to check for adequate water and feed. As they walk through, they find little of either. Henry carefully checks the eyes of each cattle he passes, finding that many are bloodshot, yellow or oozing puss. He can only shake his head with disgust and move on after a gentle pat or stroke for the doomed beast. As the group makes its way across the yard toward the plant, they come together to wind up at the opening where the cattle are led inside the building, a tall wooden structure with an open roof in the middle and various rooms where workers do their chopping and cutting. They are met by two youths wearing cowboy hats who are corralling the cattle with long prods and ushering them one by one into the killing hall.

"Who the fuck are you?" one of the boys yells out to Agent Jimmy Knickemyer, who turns to his boss just emerging from the rear. Henry steps in front of the group and replies to the boy, "We are the law, my friend. Step aside. You are about to be inspected."

The boy grabs the whistle around his neck and begins frantically blowing it. This immediately gets the attention of the workers inside. As Bergh and his men enter the facility, the workers begin whooping, booing and cat-calling, which brings out the owners with little delay. Elmer Davis looks around from his perch on a second floor and sees Bergh's men spreading out to surround the premises. He is incensed. He hightails it down the rickety wooden staircase, where he rushes to the first one of Bergh's men in uniform that he sees and pulls him by the arm and swings him around before the agent can enter a cutting room. The man shoves Davis aside and barges toward the room with unstoppable determination while the workers begin picking up animal parts strewn about on the floor and throwing the bloody organs, hooves and other discarded anatomy at Henry Bergh and his men in an angry onslaught.

Henry gets hit with several of the organic missiles as he tries to dodge the flying debris and move toward Davis across what has become an angry mob attacking and wrestling with his men. "Mr. Davis!" Henry calls out to the irate owner. "Call off your men or you will all be taken into custody."

As Henry approaches him, he is knocked down from behind with the hanging carcass of a cow that has been pushed in his direction by an angry butcher. He shakes himself off and gets up. He is now dirty, covered with animal blood and without his hat, which has gotten trampled by a rush of workers wrestling with Henry's men. Davis grabs a long, heavy blade with a wooden handle from a cutting table and swings it in the air.

Henry winces and reaches into his coat and pulls out a revolver. "I'll see you in Hell before you put yourself above the law." He raises the pistol and fires one shot into the air. The bullet hits a glass window, which shatters making a loud crashing noise as the shards of glass fall on the floor behind them.

The shock of the gunshot and falling glass stops the brawl that is ensuing. Henry calls out to Davis. "Mr. Davis, this facility is in violation of the state anticruelty law, and I am ordering it closed pending a hearing tomorrow at noon." He hands Davis a summons. "You men can wash up and go home."

"How am I to pay my landlord and feed my family if you close us down?" one angry worker calls out.

"Ask Mr. Davis and his partners to show up for his hearing on time. And pray that God forgives you," Henry adds contemptuously.

Another worker chimes in, "We don't need God's forgiveness. The Bible says we have dominion over the fish in the sea and over every creeping thing. That's in the book of Genesis!"

Henry turns to the man and calmly reaches into his pocket and takes out a paper. He unfolds it and reads. "The Bible also says, 'He that killeth an ox is as if he slew a man; he that sacrificeth a lamb, as if he cut off a dog's neck. Yea, they have chosen their own ways, and their soul delighteth in their abominations.' The book of Isaiah." He folds the paper, puts it back into his pocket then turns and directs his men to gather evidence for the hearing. The confrontation is over as the workers grumble and disperse, and Davis puts the blade back on the carving table in defeat.

Henry Bergh usually returns home around six P.M. Tonight he arrives home before five P.M. to clean up the bloody mess that he is wearing from today's adventure on the West Side, as he's in no condition to conduct Society business looking like this. He tries to enter the house quietly and slip up to his bath unnoticed. As he reaches the top of the stairs, Matilda is there and scans his appearance with wide eyes. A small trickle of dried blood runs down one cheek, his hair is disheveled, one hand is wrapped with a handkerchief to cover an abrasion when he fell.

"Oh my God, Henry, what happened to you?"

"It's nothing, dear, just a minor scuffle at the stockyards."

As he walks to the bedroom, she follows him. "Minor scuffle? Look at you. Like a common ruffian with blood and soiled clothes. And your hand?"

"Just a scrape. Nothing serious," trying to minimize her alarm. He removes his soiled, blood-stained overcoat revealing a blood-stained shirt collar and heads for the bath.

"I warned you about confronting these men. You said your men would protect you. What happened?"

"My men acted nobly. We were simply outnumbered, that's all. Next time we'll bring police with us with a warrant."

"Next time! No! There cannot be a next time! This is insanity. Look at you!" she protests loudly.

Henry keeps his composure. "I am the least of the injured. These abattoirs are houses of horrors. I mean, how God-fearing humans can inflict such torture."

"Henry! I am also being tortured. You can't do this again. I'm begging you."

Her raised voice is something he is not used to. He begins washing up, trying to calm her with his composure. "Matilda, this is not just going away. Don't you see what they're doing when they disrespect me?"

"Disrespect you? This is about you?"

He now turns and elevates his voice more sternly. "No, this is about the law. I haven't gotten this far to have these men ignore me."

"Ignore you? One of them may kill you!"

"They won't kill me."

"How do you know that? It takes only one bullet, one knife, one beating. You're not a young man, Henry!"

"I cannot abandon this cause for selfish reasons, Matilda."

She follows his movements around the bathroom as he washes and dries his hands on a towel. "Even if it means your life?"

"I don't fear for my life," he says stoically.

"Well, I do! And I'm your wife. This cause is bigger than you, Henry. One man can't go up against an evil world with his eyes shut."

"Evil men need nothing more to succeed than to have good men look on and do nothing."

"So you will wear angel wings on Earth until you are wearing them in heaven?"

"If necessary."

"Stop it, Henry. How will you help the cause by being dead and buried? And what about me? Making me a widow is the least of your worries?"

"Not at all."

"It isn't worth it!" she blurts out. He is taken aback.

"Don't say that. It is worth it. But where do I draw the line? Which animals deserve protection and which do not? The work horses get my loyalty but the pigs and cattle don't? Tell me where to stop. Look into the eyes of those pitiful innocents hanging upside down with broken limbs about to be slaughtered for someone's next meal and tell them, 'Well, I'd help you there, but my wife says I'm not allowed to put your welfare ahead of mine.' Why don't people slaughter their own dinners? Because they lack the courage to do the evil deed themselves. To play God with another living, breathing being takes fortitude. Or just plain indifference. Or simply evil avarice."

Matilda starts to cry. Henry lowers his voice.

"If I make one animal less worthy than another, then I destroy everything I have worked for. You just said this cause is bigger than me. And you are exactly right. What we've started is spreading. We both know that there are other SPCAs being formed in other jurisdictions. Other laws being passed. The compassionate are waking up and saying, 'We won't look the other way any longer.' If confrontation is dangerous, we cannot give our enemies the advantage of showing our anxiety. Let the abusers know that in our society the man with the loudest voice or the fattest wallet or biggest stick is not always the one who prevails."

He takes Matilda in his arms. "You've always trusted me in the past. I promise to not make you a widow if you promise to not stop believing in me."

He lovingly gazes into her teary eyes. She raises her hand and touches him on the cheek.

On a sunny morning, Henry Bergh arrives at the breakfast table to greet his folded newspaper. He pours himself a cup of coffee from a silver pitcher and opens the paper and begins to read. Matilda is in the kitchen assisting the cook in preparing her husband's plate of scrambled eggs, biscuit and sausage links, which the cook had just taken out of the frying pan. Matilda views the meat links and sighs.

"I don't think my husband will eat these sausages again. Since he's been inspecting the slaughterhouses, his appetite for meat has declined."

"We have some fresh berries. Shall I wash some?" the cook suggests.

Taking the plate, Matilda answers, "Let's see what he says."

Matilda enters the sun-washed dining room and sets the plate down in front of her husband and kisses him on the cheek. "Good morning, dear."

"Morning, my love." He continues scanning the paper, flipping quickly through the pages until he finishes and folds it back in half and places it next to his plate where he can read it as he eats.

"What's on your agenda today," Matilda asks as she sits.

Henry looks at his breakfast and places his napkin in his lap. "This morning I'm addressing the Board of Health."

"About the slaughterhouses?"

He picks up his knife and fork and begins to eat his eggs. "Yes. The problem of putrid meat for sale persists, and there is no formal inspection system in place. Elbridge has written a bill to create one." He quietly pushes the sausages onto a side plate and continues eating his eggs and biscuit. "If we don't clean up the abattoirs, they will continue to spread sickness and death. A six-year-old child on Fourth Avenue was pronounced dead just yesterday from trichinosis."

"Would you like some berries?" she asks.

"No, thank you. This is fine."

"You've had quite a fight with those German butchers, haven't you?"

"They're not all German. But they don't want to listen, even after they've lost one of their own."

"What do you mean?"

"A butcher named George Temple from Boston died of blood poisoning last month. It appears that he used the same towel that he washed down a dead ox he was preparing for market to wipe the sweat from his face and inflamed a sore on his cheek. The infection spread and the ignorant man died within a few days. The Boston markets had sold half of the ox before they discovered the man's death was due to blood poisoning from the ox."

"Oh, dear."

"You can imagine the furor it created when it was reported in the Boston papers."

"The same thing could happen here, couldn't it?"

"No doubt it could," Henry opines while finishing his breakfast biscuit and taking one last sip of coffee. The sausage links remain on the small plate. He looks at them. "You know, Matilda, I've always considered myself a vegetarian in the abstract, even if the rest of society will be loath to join me."

"But sometimes you eat meat," his wife points out.

"I do so reluctantly and out of habit, yes. But why should a creature condemned to death in order to nourish and sustain human life lose all claim to the merciful consideration of its slayers? The manner of all slaughter I have witnessed is appalling."

"Let's not talk about it at breakfast, Henry."

"Yet I still cannot rectify my desire to eat meat with my campaign for livestock reform. I am a hypocrite. Reverend Prine was right."

"You're a human being, Henry."

He rises, "Demanding that my *filet de boeuf* be cooked well done leaving no taint of blood is the act of a coward. We avert our gazes to cruelty when it's in our own selfish interests. That is what a human being is."

Henry kisses his wife on the cheek and leaves as Matilda ponders his statement. He travels down to City Hall by carriage, where he meets Elbridge Gerry at the steps of the County Courthouse located directly behind City Hall and also known as the Tweed Courthouse after the Democratic Party powerbroker William M. "Boss" Tweed. From there the two men walk up the granite steps and into the meeting room of the recently formed Metropolitan Board of Health, which is comprised of the Health Commissioner and four medical doctors who convene periodically in a drab meeting room across the street from City Hall to address the health and sanitation issues facing their city.

Poor sanitation and filthy streets threaten both the physical health of the public as well as the economic welfare of the developing metropolis at this time. The sanitation and city sewage is controlled by the political stronghold of Tammany Hall, which had recently nominated City Street Inspector Francis I. A. Boole for mayor. But Boole's name was soon after withdrawn when reformists discovered that street cleaning was deeply embedded in corruption, exposing the fact that workers were paid by Tammany Hall below minimum wage and forced to sign contracts that gave up half of their paycheck to Boole.

The city was under such poor management that less than two years ago one Board of Health official wrote in a three-hundred-page document entitled, *Inspection of Tenement Living*: "The streets were uncleaned; manure heaps containing thousands of tons occupied piers and vacant lots; sewers were obstructed; houses were crowded and badly ventilated and lighted; privies were unconnected with the sewers and overflowing; stables and yards were filled with stagnant water; and many dark and damp cellars were inhabited. The streets were obstructed, and the wharves and piers were filthy and dangerous from dilapidation; cattle were driven through the streets at all hours of the day in large numbers and endangered the lives of the people."

Having personally witnessed the filthy and unsanitary conditions in the slaughterhouses of Manhattan and Brooklyn, Henry Bergh sits before the Board of Health to propose a solution.

"Gentlemen, the filthy and unsanitary conditions at abattoirs have led to tainted meat for sale at the markets, causing sickness and death. Presently, food inspection is left up to police officers and the political appointees of Tammany Hall, and as much respect I have for Mr. Tweed and Mayor Hoffman, the present system is no system at all."

"What would you propose, Mr. Bergh?" Commissioner Jackson Schultz asks.

"Well Dr. Schultz, our attorney, Mr. Elbridge Gerry, has drafted a bill with a provision for appointing inspectors for the sanitary condition of all animals destined for human food. These special agents will not only protect the public against putrid meat for sale in our markets, but will enforce the animal protection laws from the slaughterhouse practices I have witnessed that comprise nothing less than savage murder."

"What practices are those, Mr. Bergh?"

"Pigs scalded and skinned alive. Calves hung by their heels for up to an hour before a butcher slits their throats. There is no reason why the profession of a butcher should be less merciful than the profession of a surgeon, unless the butcher himself chooses to make it a cruel and degrading one. Last month we inspected the Davis, Atwood & Crane slaughterhouse on West Thirty-ninth Street and were greeted with a rain of cows' liver and pigs' feet thrown at our agents by the butchers angered at our interference. There we discovered that hogs were killed in a manner so brutal that we at once threatened the company owners with arrest. Each hog was fastened with an iron chain around one leg and hoisted up forty feet, dislocating its leg joint, and then plunged still alive into boiling water."

Mr. Gerry adds, "The company hastily secured an injunction restraining the SPCA from interfering from the 'lawful prosecution of their business as hog slaughterers.' We appealed the ruling and Judge Larremore of the Court of Common Pleas thankfully dissolved the injunction and the Court of Appeals affirmed his decision."

Henry continues, "And then there are boxcars arriving at our yards with livestock dead and dehydrated, a shocking scenario that is repeated again and again throughout the Northeast. These animals are shipped from as far away as Texas and Oklahoma without food and water for sometimes days at a time. Sometimes they travel when the winter temperature is freezing cold or in the summer over one hundred degrees. Some arrive blind with fever and covered with sores. The manner of unloading is more brutal still, as I have personally witnessed cattle and sheep from an upper floor of the car pushed to jump onto an inlined platform six feet away where they often break their legs or land violently on their sides or backs. They arrive with bloodshot eyes and frothing mouths and anguished bellowing announcing their agony. We sent three agents to Chicago to inspect conditions at their stockyards and found the same conditions with the dead and dying taken off the cars by the thousands and unloaded with spike poles and pitchforks that pierce the hides of the animals sometimes twenty or thirty times. Our man approached one of the workers and asked if he wasn't afraid of putting out the creatures' eyes with such and he answered he didn't care if he did. The British have laws regulating the humane transportation of livestock dating back to 1822."

The board member sitting to the left of the commissioner speaks, "Mr. Bergh, it is my understanding that a federal statute was recently passed requiring food and water and ten hours of rest no less than every twenty-eight hours for all animals shipped in transit."

Henry responds, "Yes and the railroad owners got a rider introduced that exempted all trains of the Atlantic and Great Western and the Buffalo and State Line, the two routes that carry most of the traffic. The representatives of these powerful interests are on the alert in every legislative body to defeat everything tending to the public good that reaches into their pocketbooks. It allows nothing less than cruelty by wholesale to continue in ninety percent of the transports."

Dr. Schultz speaks, "We, too, are concerned about the tainted livestock issue and, as you know, have forced the removal of all city slaughterhouses at points above Fortieth Street. We welcome and will support your bill to create and fund an inspection unit and remain at your service to testify on its behalf if need be."

"Thank you, commissioner."

"Please keep us apprised as your inspection bill works its way through the legislature," Dr. Schultz assures.

"We will," Henry replies, as he picks up his hat and rises to exit.

Illus. 22 - 19th century Pullman Company livestock car

Illus. 23 - Dying and diseased cattle transported for slaughter

CHAPTER 10

Mary Ellen has been talking for almost thirty minutes without any fatigue or hesitation. The television crew is listening intently the whole time as the camera captures her narrative. At this point, Allen interjects, "Perhaps we should take a short break, Mrs. Schutt."

"That's fine," Mary Ellen responds. "My daughter is making lunch for us when you're hungry."

To Jed, the cameraman, he tells, "Cut it." Then turning back, "Thank you. Perhaps one more segment and then we'll break for lunch." He looks to Joan sitting beside him. "Are we where we want to be?" She nods. He turns to Jed, the cameraman, "How much left in that magazine?"

He looks at the gauge and responds, "About twenty-five minutes."

Mary Ellen chimes in, "I'm getting to my story as soon as I tell you what you need to know about Mr. Bergh and what led up to our paths crossing."

"Yes, it's a fascinating story." Mary Ellen excuses herself from the room and Allen gets up for a stretch. They take a break for only a few minutes when Mary Ellen returns, and then they all take their seats and resume the interview. At Allen's direction, Jed starts the camera.

"Speed," Jed confirms.

"You were telling us about Mr. Bergh and the ASPCA," Allen prompts her.

Mary Ellen begins again, "Mr. Bergh was always publicly dressed in his long overcoat and top hat, which emphasized his imposing size. He was six-two. And the shiny gold badge he wore was specially made for him with diamonds and rubies. He enjoyed being an authority figure. But his SPCA was expensive to operate, and the state contributed only a small portion of the funds needed to operate it. Mr. Bergh's fortune could not be the only source of money paying for staff and expenses."

"So how was the Society funded?" Allen asks.

"There were some donations from the public coming in, but Mr. Bergh got lucky in the winter of 1868, two years after he got his charter."

A light snow falls as Henry Bergh, dressed in his warmest overcoat and top hat, emerges from the modest ASPCA headquarters at Broadway and Fourth Street. A horse-drawn streetcar passes by, with passengers hanging on to the front and rear platforms because the car is too crowded for them to sit inside. Bergh shakes his head in disgust.

Elbridge Gerry arrives and is excited, "Henry, some good news."

"Not for the horses that pull Mr. Vanderbilt's overloaded streetcars. What is it?"

"Do you remember a man named Louis Bonard?"

"Yes, I remember, he's a supporter of ours."

"Well, he passed away and left his entire estate to the Society. More than one hundred forty thousand dollars!"

Henry looks up, "It's not a joke from one of our friends at the newspapers?"

"No, Henry," Gerry states happily, "It's no joke."

Henry watches the overloaded streetcar ride away as he digests the news of the sizable bequest. "They blocked our bill in the legislature to limit the number of passengers these poor creatures have to pull. It's time to take on the Vanderbilts."

With the Society's newfound resources, Henry holds strategy meetings to attack the problem of the streetcar horses. He is determined to engage powerful forces who own the various streetcar lines that service New York

City. They all had one thing in common: they all made the most money when the largest number of passengers rode on their cars. The horses be damned that they had to pull the extra weight of a car designed for eighty passengers when it was crowded with more than one hundred souls, sometimes hanging on to the platforms outside of the car because even the standing room inside was full. Bergh decides to personally direct the campaign, and it will begin immediately.

The snow falls steadily at the evening rush hour as a horse-drawn streetcar approaches. It is overloaded with passengers looking to get home for supper and out of the cold. Henry Bergh, dressed in his finest overcoat, wearing his ASPCA shield over his breast pocket and accompanied by two agents, steps out in the street and walks into the path of an oncoming streetcar and holds his hands up to stop. The surprised driver pulls on the reins and the car stops. Henry steps to the side and calls out to the driver.

"You there. Unload the passengers who don't have seats."

"In this weather? Not a chance, Mister," the driver responds.

Henry steps in closer, "Do as I say in the name of the law or my men will take you into custody." The uniformed agents step forward.

A male passenger hanging on to the platform rail hears this and calls out with annoyance, "Why should we get off? We paid our fare."

Henry looks at him sternly. "Those horses are overloaded. You can get on the next streetcar."

Agent Andy steps into enforcement mode, "Come on, everyone without a seat off." He begins directing very irate passengers off the streetcar and helping women down to the street.

One irascible old lady sees Henry and shouts at him, "I've heard about you. You're that meddling feller. You've got your nerve."

Henry is conciliatory. "Madam, I apologize for the inconvenience. The next streetcar will be along in a moment."

She snaps back, "And what if *it's* full? I'll catch my death of cold. At least the horses have blankets."

The street now has some two dozen people standing in the snow, looking down Broadway for the next streetcar that is nowhere to be seen. Henry walks over to the driver.

"If your company wants to carry more passengers, then put more buses in service. But, if I or any of my men see you overload your car again, you'll be standing before a judge. Tell your boss the law protects horses same as it does people." The driver resentfully snaps the reins to begin moving on.

A little later, the snow is falling hard and has filled the streets with white, as the horse-drawn streetcars trudge through. Henry's campaign has just begun, as he travels further uptown in search of other overloaded streetcars on the Fifth Avenue line. In the distance, he and his agents can be seen converging on another streetcar and stopping the driver from passing. This time, the passengers are more reluctant to get off due to the more severe weather. Some of them argue and make hostile gestures at the agents, as the driver gets into an argument with Henry. He gestures to his agents that they arrest the obstinate driver. They pull him out of the streetcar and handcuff him, as Henry blows a whistle to summon the police.

To date, this is Henry Bergh's boldest challenge to animal abusers. He's now going up against big companies owned by powerful men, but Henry is not fazed. The following day he fires off a letter of demand to Commodore Vanderbilt himself, who owns the Fourth and Fifth Avenue bus lines, to obey the laws protecting animals.

At the bus company's executive office, Bill McCauley, a vice president, is reading from a paper to Frederick Wilson, another executive. "Please inform the Vanderbilts that our society is charged with enforcing the laws against cruelty to animals and your company drivers will continue to be stopped and arrested if they continue to overload your streetcars. Further, if your company refuses to cease and desist this unlawful practice, the company executives in charge, including Commodore Vanderbilt himself, may face criminal prosecution. Guide yourselves accordingly. Sincerely, Henry Bergh, president."

The stunned listener responds, "You'd better bring this to the commodore immediately. Frankly, I don't want to be in the building when he reads it."

Seventy-six-year-old Cornelius Vanderbilt is likely the wealthiest man in America, having built the vast majority of his wealth in shipping and railroads. Born in Staten Island, New York, Vanderbilt began working on his father's ferry in New York Harbor as a boy, quitting school at the age of eleven. At the age of sixteen, the younger Vanderbilt decided to start his own ferry service to New Jersey with money he borrowed from his mother. One by one, he started lines between New York and the surrounding region, including the Hudson River and Long Island Sound. It was in the 1830s when he was first referred to as "commodore," then the highest rank in the United States Navy. A common nickname for important steamboat entrepreneurs, the title appealed to Vanderbilt's ego, and by the 1840s he began using it exclusively.

As the United States experienced an industrial revolution, textile mills were built in large numbers in New England. Some of the first railroads in the United States were built from Boston to Long Island Sound to connect with steamboats that ran to New York. In less than a decade, Vanderbilt dominated the steamboat business on Long Island Sound and began to take over the management of the connecting railroads, where he was a ruthless businessman, eventually taking over the New York, Providence and Boston Railroad, Erie Railway, the Central Railroad of New Jersey, the Hartford and New Haven and the New York and Harlem. In 1869, he directed the Harlem railroad to begin construction of the Grand Central Depot on Forty-second Street in Manhattan. It was finished in 1871 and served as his lines' terminus in New York. He sank the tracks on Fourth Avenue in a cut that later became a tunnel, and Fourth Avenue became Park Avenue. From there, horse-drawn trains, or trolleys, continued farther downtown. Those are the lines Henry Bergh complains are being overloaded with passengers.

A short time later, in Commodore Vanderbilt's office, the troops have been gathered around his desk. Vanderbilt holds Bergh's letter. "We've been reading about this Henry Bergh for enough years now that he is becoming a public hero. That's a problem when he opposes our activities."

"He has his supporters and his detractors," one executive chimes in.

"What are his weaknesses?" Vanderbilt wants to know. "Let's exploit them."

Another executive adds, "Mr. Bergh has compassion for the animals, but seems to lack compassion for humans."

The first executive agrees, "Yes, the public would not like Mr. Bergh if he were kind to animals but cruel to, say, a child or an elderly lady."

Food for thought.

At St. Luke's Hospital, Vanderbilt's first executive is escorting Mr. Alvin Wickes, a reporter from the *New York Star,* down the hallway as they talk.

"Your paper has been very fair in its criticisms of Mr. Bergh and his society, Mr. Wickes," Vanderbilt's toady gushes.

"The man is a zealot," the hard-nosed reporter shoots back. "The *New York Star* is only presenting the other side of the story in the interest of fairness."

They stop outside glass doors marked "Influenza Ward" and greet Dr. Hatton.

"Mr. Wickes, this is Mrs. Regan's physician, Dr. Hatton."

"Pleased to meet you, doctor. What is Mrs. Regan's condition?" the reporter inquires.

"She has acute influenza as a result of exposure," Dr. Hatton answers. "It's quite serious. At her age, if she makes it she will be very lucky."

"May I speak to her?" Wickes requests.

"Not at this time."

"I'll need to see her," he insists.

The doctor points through the glass opening in the door. "You can see her from here. She's the patient in the second bed on the right."

Wickes peers into the ward where an old lady lies in bed asleep in a ward of twenty other similar cases.

That night, braving the chilly weather, a newsboy hawks the late edition on a street corner, as bundled up New Yorkers make they way home for supper. "Get your *New York Star*, folks! Read all about it! Elderly bus rider holds on to dear life. Husband blames Animal Protection Society!"

In Henry Bergh's office the next day, Bergh, Gerry and some of the SPCA officers are gathered round a large conference table. Bergh holds the *New York Star* with the headline, "Has Animal Society Gone Too Far?" The subheadline reads, "Elderly bus passenger removed by Henry Bergh fights influenza."

Henry is reflective. "No doubt, we will lose supporters from this campaign, but it's not all bad news." He puts it down and picks up the *Tribune* with a headline, "A Triumph for Mr. Bergh" with the subheadline, "Overcrowded Street Cars Stopped, The Third Avenue Line Blockaded for Two Hours, An Extraordinary Scene, A Lesson in Cruelty to Animals."

Henry puts down the papers. "For every supporter lost from this campaign, we'll gain two new ones, but Vanderbilt and other bus company owners will plot to discredit us further."

Elbridge asks, "What happens if the old lady dies? They will want your head, Henry."

"I'm not worried. She won't die. She's the mother of the commodore's brother-in-law. Nice detective work, Andy." Bergh acknowledges his agent, who nods his head in return.

"They will likely sue the Society for tortious interference," Elbridge adds.

"Bring them on, counsellor."

"Our record in court is only modestly successful," the attorney notes.

"We may not always prevail when we sue the animal abusers, but we have never lost a case when you have had to defend the Society. And the bigger the case, the more the newspapers air our grievances in the public arena. With that in mind, we received a letter of complaint about that damned P.T. Barnum and his so-called Museum and Menagerie. He's at it again. Let me read it to you."

Mary Ellen is filled with energy as she tells Henry Bergh's story. "Mr. Bergh was never afraid of going against anyone who abused or misused animals. And the more powerful they were, the harder Mr. Bergh pushed back. That was the case when the great showman P.T. Barnum was lined up in Mr. Bergh's crosshairs. They got into a terrible feud that practically drove Mr. Bergh crazy."

The notorious and spectacular P.T Barnum came from humble beginnings to become a household name in America by cultivating the art of promotion. Standing six feet two inches tall, with curly receding hair above wide innocent blue eyes, a bulbous nose, cleft chin and a high-pitched voice, Barnum is a bombastic and relentless bundle of energy. Often referred to as the "Prince of Humbugs," Barnum saw nothing wrong in using hype or "humbug," as he termed it, to promote his ventures. And the more outrageous the claims, the more audiences flocked to see his shows and exhibitions. Although Barnum was also an author, publisher, lecturer, philanthropist, real estate speculator and, for some time, a politician, he said of himself, "I am a showman by profession...and all the gilding shall make nothing else of me." His personal aims were simply "to put money in the coffers." He is credited with introducing the modern public museum, the popular concert and the three-ring circus.

Born in Bethel, Connecticut, Phineas Taylor Barnum became a small-business owner in his early twenties, founded a weekly newspaper and ran a general store where he helped set up and profit from one of the first statewide lottery networks. In 1834, when lotteries were banned in Connecticut, cutting off his main income, Barnum sold his store and moved to New York City. He embarked on an entertainment career in 1835 with his purchase and exhibition of a blind and almost completely paralyzed slave woman, Joice Heth, whom Barnum claimed to have been George Washington's nurse and to be over one hundred sixty years old. When she died the next year at age eighty, he went on to a year of mixed success with his first variety troupe called Barnum's Grand Scientific and Musical Theater. The Panic of 1837, a financial crisis that touched off a major recession that lasted a decade, resulted in three years of difficulty for Barnum. Then in

1841, he purchased Scudder's American Museum at Broadway and Ann Street. He improved the attraction, renamed it Barnum's American Museum, upgrading the building and adding exhibits, and it became a popular showplace. Barnum added a lighthouse lamp that attracted attention up and down Broadway and flags along the roof's edge that attracted attention in daytime. From between the upper windows, giant paintings of animals drew stares from pedestrians. The roof was transformed to a strolling garden with a view of the city, where he launched hot-air balloon rides daily. Barnum used the museum as a platform to promote hoaxes and human curiosities such as the "Feejee" mermaid, which was actually the torso and head of a baby monkey sewn to the back half of a fish and covered in papier-mâché, and General Tom Thumb, a two-foot, eleven-inch man. A changing series of live acts and curiosities, including albinos, giants, midgets, "fat boys," jugglers, magicians, exotic women, detailed models of cities and famous battles and, eventually, a menagerie of animals were added to the exhibits of stuffed animals.

Like many New Yorkers, Henry was familiar with Barnum's activities for years. In fact, in 1850 when Barnum promoted the American tour of singer Jenny Lind, paying her an unprecedented thousand dollars a night for one hundred fifty nights, Henry and Matilda were in the audience at the Castle Garden to hear the "Swedish Nightingale" perform. Twenty years later, Bergh's and Barnum's paths would cross over the showman's use of live animals.

After a decade of modest success for Herman Mellville's *Moby-Dick: or The White Whale*, Barnum was inspired by a report he read about a live white whale being captured by fishermen at the mouth of the St. Lawrence River. Barnum was determined to have his own white whale exhibit, and so he began construction in the basement of his museum a brick and cement tank eighteen feet wide by fifty feet long. He then set out to Canada, where he hired two dozen French Canadian fishermen to capture male and female specimens, offering a generous bonus if they could capture a pair. Shortly after returning to New York, Barnum got word that the fishermen were successful, and he arranged a private freight car be sent to transport his sea mammals on their five-day journey to New York. Each white whale rested uncomfortably in a crate filled with salt water and seaweed, attended by a Barnum employee who continually wet down the animal with sea water. The trip was accompanied by a ceaseless barrage of publicity. Hourly dispatches were fed to the press, and a stream of bulletins were posted to the museum, so that when the animals arrived, "anxious thousands literally rushed to see the strangest curiosities ever exhibited in New York," Barnum proudly announced. When the mammals arrived they were lowered into the basement tank that had been filled with fresh water artificially salted. Barnum described his first foray into such an exhibition thusly, "My first whaling expedition was a great success, but I did not know how to feed or take care of the monsters, and, moreover, they were in fresh water, and this, with the bad air of the basement, may have hastened their death, which occurred a few days after their arrival, but not before thousands of people had seen them."

Encouraged by the large crowds of spectators who each paid twenty-five cents, Barnum was determined to repeat and improve the exhibit and reap another windfall profit. And so he again commissioned Canadian fishermen to capture another pair of white whales while he constructed a new tank on the second floor of the museum at a cost of four thousand dollars. This tank was larger and had a pipe leading to the river supplying a steady stream of real salt water. In a short time, two more white whales were installed. "It was a great sensation," Barnum reported, "and it added thousands of dollars to my treasury. The whales, however, soon died. Their sudden and immense popularity was too much for them."

Undiscouraged, Barnum ordered a third pair at a cost of ten thousand dollars. Barnum's advertising declared, "I am highly gratified," one notice concluded, "in being able to assure the public that they have arrived safe and well, a male and female, from 15 to 20 feet long, and are now swimming in the miniature ocean in my museum, to the delight of visitors. As it is very doubtful whether these wonderful creatures can be kept alive more than a few days, the public will see the importance of seizing the first moment to see them."

A reporter from Greeley's *Tribune* observed them in seven feet of water, but went on to extoll the marvel of such display anyway. After the first whale died, the *Tribune* blamed the catastrophe on "the foul scent of a resentful grizzly bear" and ran a lengthy obituary lamenting Mr. Barnum's loss as "a shocking reminder of the emptiness of all human plans." Such was the indifferent attitude of the public just a few years before the formation of Henry Bergh's ASPCA. After the demise of the second whale, Barnum would go on to replace the empty tank with a three-year-old hippopotamus from Africa, followed in turn by sharks, sea horses, angel fish and porpoises. But in June of 1865, the wood-framed American Museum burned to the ground with its inhabitants inside. To Barnum, it was merely a financial loss. Within six months, Barnum reopened his New American Museum on the west side of Broadway between Spring and Prince Streets after renovating the old Chinese Museum. He again stocked a menagerie with lions and tigers, the only giraffe in North America, the smallest elephant found in Africa and, in partnership with Van Amburgh Menagerie

Company, the animal Barnum most desired, a huge and ferocious African gorilla, which drew large crowds. When a professor visiting the exhibit pointed out that it was no gorilla at all, but a baboon, Barnum wanted to know how he knew that. When the professor pointed out that ordinary gorillas have no tails, Barnum's response was, "But mine has, and that makes the specimen more remarkable."

James Gordon Bennett of the *Herald* was the only publisher who recognized Barnum for what he was and became a perpetual adversary. Barnum didn't seem to mind the attacks, writing, "I always found Bennett's abuse far more remunerative than his praise, when I could be the subject of his scolding editorials free of charge instead of paying him forty cents a line for advertisements which would not attract a tenth part so much attention." Barnum did not feel the same way about Henry Bergh when Bergh began to notice Barnum's indifferent and abusive treatment of the live animals in his exhibitions. It takes a letter from a member of the public appalled at what he saw at Barnum's Menagerie to begin an investigation.

On a bustling Friday night in New York, Bergh and Gerry stand outside the ornate wooden Hippodrome building on Broadway and Fourteenth Street, site of Barnum's third Broadway Museum and Menagerie. As they pass the various posters advertising the show housed within, Agent Andy emerges from the building.

"Well?" Henry awaits the agent's report.

"From what I could see, I estimate there are a little more than two hundred live animals inside. And the boa constrictor feeding was just as the gentleman described. The bunny was placed in the center of the cage, it saw the snake and cowered to the corner, shivering in terror as the snake slowly approached it."

"And the crowd?" Bergh asks.

"Some were delighted, others uncomfortable. No one complained to the animal handler," Andy answers.

"It's barbaric," Henry snorts.

Gerry chimes in, "We'll issue our cease and desist letter directly to Mr. Barnum."

"And what about this wooden fire-hazard? It's already burned twice before. Who knows how many animals were lost each time?" Henry asks his attorney.

"One issue at a time, Henry. Let's see how receptive Mr. Barnum is to our criticism."

Henry goes home and has a late meal alone as Matilda wasn't feeling well and had gone into the bedroom to lie down. After dinner, Henry goes to the parlor to engage in an activity he tries to make a weekly chore, pasting newspaper clippings into a scrapbook. He takes the kerosene lamp to the table and sits, where a stack of papers awaits him. With scissors and mucilage, he cuts the various articles and cartoons from the papers and begins pasting them into a large scrapbook. He rereads every article first and sometimes annotates them with underlines or notes in the margin. As he looks at one and shakes his head, Matilda enters.

"Come to bed, Henry. It's getting late."

"Look what they say about me, Matilda, that I'm 'a maudlin sympathizer with persecuted rats and unfortunate bedbugs.' The *Mercury* calls me a 'humbug' for opposing cockfights."

"Henry," she tries to console him.

"And when I stopped them from drowning dogs in the East River, *Puck* said I was 'the only mourner.'" He shows her a cartoon from *Puck* with a caricature of himself weeping into a handkerchief while following the dogcatcher's wagon filled with dogs.

"That's not true and you know it. Your work is changing laws and changing minds. You're doing the work of angels," she insists.

Henry is not to be consoled. "Sometimes it bedevils me."

"Let the cynics say what they will. Don't play into their hands," Matilda advises.

"Today we filed a prosecution of a dealer who mixed marble dust in his horse feed. Where does it end? The more I see of men, the more I admire dogs."

Matilda bends down and comforts her husband.

Illus. 24 - Henry Bergh stops a streetcar in
Harpers Weekly's "The Crowded Car" drawn by Sol Eytinge, Jr.

Illus. 25 - sometimes streetcars were carrying
double their legal capacity

Illus. 26 - Phineas Taylor "P.T." Barnum

Illus. 27 - Barnum's American Museum

Illus. 28 - Puck portrays Bergh as *"The only mourner"* following the dog catcher's cart to the city pound

THE ARREST, (AFTERWARDS IMPRISONMENT,) FOR KILLING A CAT, ALTHOUGH PROVOKED TO THE ACT BY A CAT-NIP
(*Respectfully* DED-I-CAT-ED *is the man of* YELLS (?)—*Mr. N. Rodburg, President of the Society for the Prevention of Foolery about Animals.*)

Illus. 29 - Bergh satirized for arresting a cat-killing family man

CHAPTER 11

Henry Bergh is determined to butt heads with the fabulous P.T. Barnum over his live feedings of the boa constrictor that is nothing less than an assault on civilized men. When Barnum ignores his protest, he sits at his desk and writes a letter to the managers of Barnum's Museum:

December 11, 1866
Gentlemen:

I some time since called at Barnum's Museum for the purpose of protesting against the cruel mode of feeding the snake, which is there on exhibition. The gentleman, whom I spoke with, who informed me that he was acting for Mr. Barnum in his absence, expressed his willingness to use his influence to have the evil corrected.

Nothing, it seems has been done in that direction, as I am this moment informed by a gentleman who was present some four weeks ago that he witnessed the feeding of the animal, along with other spectators, and pronounced the scene cruel and demoralizing in the extreme; several live animals having been thrown into its cage, to be slowly devoured!

I boast of no finer sensibilities than other men, but I assert, without fear of contradiction, that any person who can commit an atrocity such as the one I complain of is semi-barbarian in his instincts. It is with a view to prevent and punish such offenses that this society has been created and laws enacted.

It may be urged that these reptiles will not eat dead food—in reply to this I have to say, then let them starve—for it is contrary to the merciful providence of God that wrong should be committed in order to accomplish a supposed right.

But, I am satisfied that this assertion is false in theory and practice, for no living creature will allow itself to perish of hunger, with food before it, be the aliment dead or alive.

I therefore am led to the conclusion that this cruel deed is a part of the spectacle; in total disregard of the demoralizing effects of it, or the inhumanity, which results therefrom.

I have therefore respectfully to apprise you that on the next occurrence of this cruel exhibition, this Society will take legal measures to punish the perpetrators of it.

Please let me hear from you without delay.

Your obedient servant,

Henry Bergh, President

When the letter arrived at its destination, the managers of Mr. Barnum's Museum read it with amusement. "Old man Bergh is really gonna rile the boss with this one," the senior manager, one Julius Blackstone, declares to his immediate subordinate, the strikingly smug Harry Stilwell, after reading the letter aloud.

"Oh balls, the old man isn't going to give two shakes of a dead lamb's tail about such shit," Stilwell spews back. "I'll put it on his desk."

On Barnum's desk is where the letter sat for two and a half months before Mr. Barnum got around to answering it. Barnum knew the consequences of ignoring Bergh's threats and waited until such time that he could accumulate some ammunition to rebut Mr. Bergh's allegations.

New York, March 4, 1867

Henry Bergh, Esq.

Dear Sir:

On my return from the West in December last, I found your letter of December 11, addressed to this association, threatening us with punishment if we permitted our boa constrictors to eat their food alive. You furthermore declared that our assertion that these reptiles would die unless permitted to eat their food alive was "false in theory and practice, for no living creature will allow itself to perish with hunger, with food before it, be the aliment dead or alive." I enclose a letter from Professor Agassiz, denying your statement.

In addition to threatening us with prosecution, you take it upon yourself to denounce us as "semi-barbarians," simply because we choose to conduct our business in the only way which we believe will be satisfactory to that public, who expect to see animals here as nearly in their natural state as they can be exhibited. I, sir, was much rejoiced at the establishment of your society, and believe it can do a world of good in saving dumb animals from abuse, but in the present instance you are unquestionably in the wrong, and I give you notice that this establishment will continue to feed all its animals in accordance with the laws of nature.

If upon reflection, you think proper to write us a letter for publication, stating that since reading Professor Agassiz's letter to us, you withdraw your objections, that will satisfy us. Otherwise we shall feel compelled to self-defense to publish your former letter in connection with that from Professor Agassiz.

Truly yours,
P.T. Barnum
President of Barnum's and Van Amburgh's Museum and Menagerie

The following letter from Prof. Louis Agassiz to P.T. Barnum is enclosed in the above letter to Bergh:

Cambridge, February 28, 1867
P.T. Barnum, Esq., New York
Dear Sir:
On my return to Cambridge I received your letter of the 15th of January. I do not know of any way to induce

snakes to eat their food otherwise than in their natural manner: that is alive. Your museum is intended to show to the public the animals, as nearly as possible, in their natural state. The society of which you speak is, I understand, for the prevention of unnecessary cruelty to animals. It is a most praiseworthy object, but I do not think the most active member of the society would object to eating lobster salad because the lobster was boiled alive or refuse roasted oysters because they were cooked alive or raw oysters because they must be swallowed alive.

I am, dear sir, your obedient servant,
L.E. Agassiz

When the letters arrive at ASPCA headquarters, Henry is outraged at first, but then recalls with whom he is dealing and is resigned not to let the infamous huckster get the best of him. Henry views the correspondence as a sparring match between two seasoned fighters. He sits down to compose an appropriate response.

New York, March 7, 1867
P.T. Barnum, Esq., New York
Dear Sir:
I hereby acknowledge the receipt of a letter from you on the dated the 4th of March, including one to you from Professor Agassiz, relating to the feeding of your boa constrictor on live animals.

The Society for the Prevention of Cruelty of Animals was chartered by the Legislature of this State for the purpose indicated by its title. Among the vast number of complaints made to it, imploring its interposition in behalf of suffering brute creatures, was one received from a gentleman whose name is purposely withheld but whose entire communication is at any time subject to your inspections, the salient point of which I quote below. In describing what he had witnessed at your place of amusement, he says: "A rabbit was thrust into the cage of a serpent, when it immediately rushed to the farthest corner and commenced trembling like an aspen leaf.

After some time the boa slowly brought its head so as to bring its eyes to bear upon its victim and then rested. The intense terror of the poor rabbit and its pitiable helplessness made me sick. I implored the keeper to take it out, but was laughed at for my pains. It was in the evening when the rabbit was put into the cage. I thought of it all night. The next morning I called to see if my little friend was out of its misery. The situation was unchanged. The reptile had not moved a particle. Its eyes still rested upon the rabbit, which was closely crouched in the same corner and trembling violently. In the evening I called again; still the same and the next morning still the same. At length, late in the evening of the third day, I called, and the little rabbit had seemingly fallen into a semi-stupor, from which it would arouse and open its eyes, but close them again after the manner of a man who sleeps and nods in his chair.

The serpent had moved his head a few inches nearer. When I called the next morning the little rabbit was gone. The above occurrence took place in the public exhibition room and was part of the show. If Yankee ingenuity cannot devise some other means of keeping these horrible creatures alive, I am sure we are better without the sight of them."

On the receipt of this letter, I called at your place of business, and on my representation of the case was assured by the gentlemen in charge—who appeared to be humanely inclined—that the practice should be discontinued but subsequently, a second letter having been received by me, announcing a repetition of the cruel performance, I wrote you the note referred to, in reply to which a letter was sent me by your agent again deprecating the proceeding and strongly asserting that it shall not be repeated.

Thus the matter rested until the receipt of your letter of March 4th, transmitting a threat to give my letter to the public unless "upon reflection I thought proper to write you, stating that since reading Professor Agassiz's letter to you, I withdrew my objections, etc. etc."

In reply to this I have to say that the hastily written note to which you refer was not intended for publication, but if you think any business capital can be realized from it, I have no objection to its sharing the fate of everything subjected to the ordeal of your fertile genius.

But I may, perhaps, be permitted at the same time to express the surprise I feel that so consummate an adept in the school of humbug as your self-published autobiography proves you to be should make the mistake of believing that the same public, after reading that delectable volume, would fail to see through the transparent covering with which the motive is enveloped. This, however, is your affair, not mine.

As to withdrawal of my objection, after reading Professor Agassiz's letter, I have to say that so far from discovering by the perusal of it any reason for changing my long cherished opinions of the necessity of practicing humanity to the brute creation, I am more convinced than ever of the necessity of laboring still more assiduously in that cause, in order to counteract the unhappy influence which the expressions of that justly distinguished savant is calculated to occasion. Permit me to add that I scarcely know which emotion is paramount in my mind, regret or astonishment, that so eminent a philosopher should have seemingly cast the weight of his commanding authority into the scale where cruelty points the index in its favor.

The result is obvious, therefore; the offensive letter must be published, although I predict beforehand that so doing will occasion no convulsion of nature nor otherwise disturb the repose of society, nor will it even realize for its exhibition the results anticipated; but it is possible, on the contrary, that it may cause parents and other guardians of the morals of the rising generation to discontinue conducting them to a mis-called museum, where the amusement chiefly consists in contemplating the prolonged torture of innocent, unresisting, dumb creatures.

    Your obedient servant,
    Henry Bergh

On receipt and reading of Henry's response, Barnum is both annoyed and challenged. After all, he gave Mr. Bergh an option to cease hostilities and supplied him with scientific facts, but the intemperate Mr. Bergh threw down the gauntlet and proposed to ratchet things up a notch. And the stinging personal insults are straining Barnum's genuine respect for Mr. Bergh and his cause. But, if Mr. Bergh wishes to try the case in the court of public opinion, he falls right into Barnum's modus operandi of grinding the publicity mill for all it is worth.

New York, March 11, 1867
Henry Bergh, Esquire
President of American Society for the Prevention of Cruelty to Animals
Sir:
On my return from Connecticut, for but a few hours sojourn in the city, I find your letter of March 7th. It is lamentable that a gentleman standing at the head of an institution which, if properly conducted, would command the respect and sympathy of all well-disposed persons, should be so incredulous and possess such a superficial knowledge of the subject as to be deceived by so silly and absurd a letter as you quote from. This entire story of the trembling, fearful rabbit is a shallow hoax. And the pretence that during four dark nights and three days this persistent, unwinking snake should be staring incessantly at his terrified little victim is simply a

ridiculous Munchausenism, founded upon the old story of serpent-charming birds. But no naturalist will pretend for a moment that the lazy, dull-eyed boa constrictor possesses any such power or that any bird or animal placed in his cage has the slightest instinctive admonition that he is in danger. On the contrary, pigeons jump about upon him as carelessly as if they were on the ground and roost upon his back all night as fearlessly as if he was the branch of a tree. Rabbits lie and sleep among his folds with as much unconcern as if within their own burrows. This whole story, therefore, of those long days and nights of terror and the gradual wearing out of the sleepless rabbit, reducing him to a "semi stupor like a man who sleeps and nods on his chair," is as ludicrous a piece of fiction as ever was read in the "Arabian Nights' Tales," and its publication will inevitably make you the laughingstock of every naturalist in Christendom.

Twenty-five years ago I witnessed the eventful workings in London of an institution of the same title as that of which you are president, and I have frequently urged the importance of organizing a similar society here. But sir, discretion, civility, and good judgment are requisite in securing to the objects of that institution the best results. Letters "hastily written," charging a man with being a "semi-barbarian" and haughtily threatening him with punishment for doing what no man with a well-balanced mind could imagine he had done are not, in my humble judgment, the most effective means for a person in your position to make use of. Your last letter, which seems not to have been so "hastily written," but evidently intended for the public press, is as uncharitable as it is unjust. When you attribute to me a desire to make "business capital" out of a transaction originated by yourself, wherein you have unwarrantably applied to me insulting epithets, and treated me in a most ungentlemanly manner, simply because I wished to be set right on a point wherein you have clearly attempted to place me in the wrong is not worthy of a person filling the honorable and responsible position to which you, sir, have been elected. Your vulgar allusions to "humbug" and that "delectable volume" betray low breeding and a surplus of self-conceit which will but tend to deepen the impression which many sensible and humane men have formed in regard to your unfitness for the office of "President of the American Society, etc." Your abrupt charges and sweeping insinuations are offensive and without reason. For instance, your assertion that the letter of Professor Agassiz confirms you still more in the opinion of "the necessity of practicing humanity to the brute creation," from which the public are to infer that the learned and honorable professor did not so zealously believe and practice on that belief as you do. Herein seems to be one of your greatest foibles. You apparently consider everybody "brutal" and "barbarous" and opposed to "practicing humanity" unless they agree with you in the attempt to set at defiance the laws of nature. Your dictatorial air is unsufferable, and your concluding threat that the publication of your former letter in connection with that of Professor Agassiz will drive children and their mothers away from a museum in which I have but a partial pecuniary interest, and for the financial returns of which I don't care a "tuppence" so that the public get, as usual, four times more genuine instruction and innocent amusement than they pay for, is a specimen of petty malice which will accords with the general tenor of your conduct in your new position. And then, again, your offensive and unwarrantable charges of the "insults anticipated" by me in such publication emanates only from the brain of a man mounted upon stilts, who seems to be delighted in seeing himself in print in whatever shape circumstances may place him there. When private enterprise has invested half a million of dollars and incurs a yearly disbursement of

$300,000 in which to place before the public a full representation of every department of natural history for a mere nominal sum—an enterprise never before attempted in any city in the world without governmental aid—it simply is disgraceful for you to assert that the "amusement chiefly consists in contemplating the prolonged torture of innocent and unresisting dumb creatures." How weak must a person feel his position to be when he attempts to fortify it by such thoughtless and absurd statements, and how little does he appreciate the true dignity of his office when he thus descends to miserable pettyfogging and the unjust imputation of bad motives to those who take quite as humane and much more rational view of the subject than himself. The officers of your institution, sir, are gentlemen of too much worth and command too generally the respect of the community for its president to degrade it and them by "hasty" unreflecting, and unjust deportment toward others. In attempting to prevent the abuse of beasts your influence will not be increased by your abuse of men. As you seem to court the pillory by asking for the publication of your last letter, I bow to your request, wondering at your temerity, but thinking to use your own language, "It is your affair, not mine." Of course no public officer like yourself has a right to consider his official orders as "private" and exempt from publication. The public all have an interest in the proper management of a society for the prevention of cruelty to animals and have a right to know whether its chief officer is fit for his position.

Your arbitrary conduct, however, compelled my associates to send their reptiles to a neighboring state to be fed; but we shall have no more such tomfoolery until driven to it by that legal decision which you threaten and to which we most willingly appeal.

Your obedient servant,
P.T. Barnum

A letter from Barnum to the *Evening Post* followed.

American Museum, June 22, 1867
To the Editors of the Evening Post:
Your paper of yesterday gives a remedy, proposed by the London Punch, *to meet the objection of the president of "The Society for the Prevention of Cruelty to Animals" to feeding serpents in the only manner which nature permits. Mr. Punch may overcome English sensitiveness by rejecting live rabbits as food for the boas constrictor and substituting "Welsh rabbits" in their places. But Shakespeare tells us of "maggot ostentation" and from my experience with the tender susceptibilities of Mr. Bergh, I tremble lest the keen scent of that gentleman might enable him to smell danger to animal suffering by that process, and that he would, therefore, offer a small mite of objection even to feeding serpents upon toasted cheese!*
Truly yours,
P.T. Barnum

Barnum was not the only public adversary Henry Bergh would engage, as he was not one to shy away from controversy or outspoken critics, even when his critic was a member of the clergy. Henry was raised a Unitarian, as several of the Founding Fathers were, but at heart he was a secular humanist. God was a concept he could accept, but organized religion was not. There were too many religious people who did terrible things to animals and people alike and still called themselves disciples of Jesus, the Prince of Peace.

So when the publisher of the *New York Observer*, Rev. Dr. Irenaeus Prine, was writing stories critical of Mr. Bergh's unwavering defense of all living creatures, Henry got irritated enough to fire off a letter to the good reverend, challenging him to a debate. Not to his surprise, Prine accepted. Through his friendship with Peter Cooper, Henry secured the Great Hall at the

Cooper Union Building, one of New York's premier meeting places located at Astor Place, as the site for the debate.

Henry's friend Peter Cooper, who was a signer for the SPCA's original charter, founded the Cooper Union for the Advancement of Science and Art in 1859 as a private college with an egalitarian goal that an education "equal to the best" should be available to everyone irrespective of race, religion, sex, wealth or social status, which was a radical concept at that time.

Cooper was a prolific inventor, successful entrepreneur and one of America's richest businessmen of his day, despite being a workingman's son who had less than a year of formal schooling. He designed and built America's first steam railroad engine, made his fortune with a glue factory and iron foundry and was also successful in real estate, insurance, railroads and telegraphy. He once ran for President under the Greenback Party, being the oldest candidate ever nominated for a presidential election.

On February 27, 1860, the school's Great Hall, located in the basement level of the Foundation Building, became the site of a historic address by presidential candidate Abraham Lincoln, opposing Stephen A. Douglas on the question of federal power to regulate and limit the spread of slavery to the federal territories and new states, a speech that was widely reported and galvanized support for Lincoln and contributed to his gaining the Republican Party's nomination.

"Debate between Rev. Dr. Irenaeus Prine, editor of the *New York Observer*, and Mr. Henry Bergh, president of the American Society for the Prevention of Cruelty to Animals," was the sign posted outside Cooper Union's Great Hall, as a variety of spectators from the well-dressed to students and even a cadre of medical doctors filed in to take their seats. The gas lamps were turned up to their highest illumination so the audience could see Henry and Rev. Prine enter the stage clearly and take their positions at two wooden lecterns.

Professor Wilson from the school introduced the two debaters, and Rev. Prine was given first place to speak.

"The Bible states that man shall have dominion over the animals, does it not, Mr. Bergh?"

Henry responds without hesitation, "It does, but one must define 'dominion,' Reverend Prine. Is such dominion conferred as human dominance over the animals or as a benevolent stewardship of them? I say it is the latter."

"Mr. Bergh, you have permitted your SPCA agents to endanger the health of a lady by holding up her carriage on a snowy day until a sound horse could be substituted for her lame beast. Is that not carrying your campaign for animals at the expense of human well-being?"

"Reverend Prine, I take exception with your doctrine that the life and health of one human being are of more value in the sight of God than all the horses in New York. The Almighty entertains no discriminating partiality for any of His creatures. The insect in the plant, the moth hovering about the candle's flame, even the life which inhabits a drop of water is as much an object of the Lord's special Providence as the mightiest king on his throne."

Prine responds, "Humans suffer at the hands of humans right here in our very city. We allow notorious slums to produce crime-breeding saloons and dance halls, populating our overcrowded city jails. Do not men suffer languishing in our jails, Mr. Bergh?"

"They have it better in our jails than in Cairo, where I visited the court where petty criminals were tried. I have seen men thrown on their faces for petty crimes and given a licking with the whip. They squirmed and shrieked and called on Allah to witness they would never offend any more. And they were morally improved. That is the kind of suffering I advocate."

Prine perks up, "But what manner is this? The leader of the Society for the Prevention of Cruelty to Animals, a man who would weep for an overladen cart horse, but watch approvingly while blood runs to the ground from a fellow man whose tender back is being cut to ribbons?"

Henry is not contrite, "I have no sympathy for the maudlin nonsense of pampering criminals. The old-fashioned whipping post is the scourge for minor offenders. I would even go so far as offer a reward for the inventor of a steam-powered whipping machine whose impartial justice could not be bribed."

The audience roars with laughter.

Prine is not amused, "Is that not hypocrisy, sir!"

"No, sir. God gave the animal feeling and the man reason. If the man abuses his powers, he should be made to suffer. Drivers who brutally flog their horses in the streets of our city, slaughterhouse butchers and cruelists in the sporting rings cannot be led to kindly habits by moral suasion. Such men, with brutal passions and blunted intellects, can only be taught humanity by fear."

"And you are called by the Lord to administer justice to such men?" Prine asks.

Henry snaps back, "No, my powers are conferred upon me by the state to terrify the workers of cruelty. I only regret that the Legislature that passed our SPCA's anti-cruelty to animals statute failed to give us the power to inflict punishment. I should like to see the law changed so that the man who beats his horse should be more severely punished than the common pickpocket. And cockfighters be pounded until their skins are as black as their hearts."

The audience applauds enthusiastically. The debate goes on for some fifty minutes. At its conclusion, Henry feels satisfied that he has adequately defended Rev.

Prine's reactionary charges, and the audience appears to have agreed.

That week, *Puck* published a satirical cartoon of Henry tied down to a bench while receiving blows to the rear from a steam-powered mechanized paddle machine, punishment "for cruelty to men." When Henry sees it in his morning papers, he can do little more than shake his head forlornly.

The light in Mary Ellen's sunroom has changed as the noonday sun travels overhead. Jed, the cameraman, signals to Allen, his producer, that the camera needs attention.

"We'll need to take a break to change the film in our camera," Allen tells Mary Ellen.

"Of course," she acknowledges.

"Mrs. Schutt," Joan addresses her.

"Please, call me Mary Ellen," she implores.

"Thank you. Mary Ellen, Mr. Bergh seems like a larger than life person. I had no idea of his accomplishments."

Jed chimes in while reloading the camera, "Yeah, the guy really knew how to kick butt."

Mary Ellen looks up surprised and disapprovingly.

Joan shoots Jed a look of disapproval, and he sheepishly apologizes, "Sorry."

"Forgive him, he was raised in Brooklyn," Joan explains.

Mary Ellen continues, "Mr. Bergh was totally committed to reform and knew all the influential people of his day. That's why he was able to help me."

"Would you like to take a break now?" Allen asks.

"No. I like talking to you. Tell me, do you know Dinah Shore?"

Allen is taken by surprise, "Well, no. She's on another network."

"I think she's lovely," Mary Ellen says. "I hope I'm not using up too much of your film to tell about Mr.

Bergh's life. I will get to where our paths crossed very soon."

Joan responds, "No, that's quite all right."

Jed has finished changing the camera's film magazine and adjusts the floodlight so it is not so directed at his subject under the increased noonday sun and announces, "I'm ready." He puts on his headphones, turns on the camera and then nods to Allen.

"Good. Let's continue then," Allen responds.

Mary Ellen continues her story, "Mr. Bergh moved the Society to new and larger headquarters as the Society grew."

A light snow falls as workers are moving furniture into a limestone building on the corner of Fourth Avenue and Twenty-second Street, home of the new ASPCA Building. They carry furnishings into the entrance past a shiny new embossed plaque with the letters A.S.P.C.A. around a bas relief emblem with horses being driven by a teamster over whom an angel hovers. Above the front doors a worker is installing a sign that reads "American Society for the Prevention of Cruelty to Animals."

Henry Bergh, dressed in his warmest overcoat and top hat, stands near the curb observing the scene. Elbridge Gerry enters with a newspaper in hand.

"Have you seen Mr. Barnum's letter in the *World*?" Gerry asks.

Henry answers, "No."

Gerry hands him the paper. Bergh reads wide-eyed, then looks up. "They published my letter, too?" Gerry nods.

Henry reads, "In addition to threatening us with prosecution, you take it upon yourself to denounce us as 'semi-barbarians.'" Henry mumbles to himself then continues. "I, sir, was much rejoiced at the establishment of your society, and believe it can do a world of good in saving dumb animals from abuse, but in the present instance you are unquestionably in the wrong, and this establishment will continue to feed all its animals in accordance with the laws of nature."

Gerry adds, "He cites Professor Agassiz's opinion that the feeding was consistent with the natural order of these species."

"The spectacle of the feeding is outrageous. If he wants to try this case in the newspapers, we'll accommodate him," Henry declares and then turns and enters the building with a determined gait. Gerry just shakes his head.

Henry spends the afternoon composing yet another letter to P.T. Barnum that the famous showman would not be able to refute. It's a delicate balance of acknowledging that there is cruelty in nature weighed against man inflicting similar treatment in captive and unnatural settings. Agent Tommy Childs knocks and enters the room.

"Mr. B, we just got a complaint that a horse is standing out in the snow with no blanket in front of a store on Broadway and Reade."

"You get a blanket and I'll prepare a summons."

"Yes, sir."

Henry looks out the window to view the inclement weather. He gathers up a summons and his warmest overcoat and hastily accompanies his trusted agent out of the office to rush to the scene before the horse freezes to death.

The snow is falling heavily as the two men arrive at a harness shop on the corner of Broadway and Reade Streets where a horse is standing silently in the storm. As Bergh and Childs approach the horse, they see a sign affixed to the side of the horse advertising the Gotham Harness Shop. On closer examination, the words are painted on the horse, which is made of wood. Bergh and Child turn to each other, realizing they've been duped. Their return to headquarters is a humiliating one.

PUCK'S CONCEPTION OF MR. BERGH'S STEAM FLOGGING MACHINE.

Illus. 30 - Puck satirizes Bergh's idea for punishment

CHAPTER 12

Funerals have always been events that Henry Bergh avoided. That's why it is so unsettling that Henry finds himself on a rainy day in a country cemetery listening to the eulogy of someone named Mr. Licorice whom he can't remember ever meeting. The mourners dressed in black are weeping profusely as the rain comes steadily down on a sea of umbrellas. Henry is without an umbrella and stands in the rain, holding together the collar of his overcoat to stay warm as the raindrops cascade over the brim of his top hat. The minister extolls the virtues of the deceased as a noble and inspirational being. Henry looks to his left and then to his right, but he doesn't recognize anyone around him.

A clap of thunder resonates ominously, punctuating the uncomfortable and disoriented feeling coming over Henry. Why is he here? Who is the deceased? Why doesn't he know? Feeling misplaced, Henry decides to leave the scene, and as he turns to walk away, a beautiful dark-haired woman walks up to him and hands him a flower. As he looks at it, she leans forward and kisses him on the cheek and then turns and walks toward a hearse coach pulled by two white horses. Perplexed, Henry decides to follow her. He feels a tug on his coattail and turns to find a little girl wearing a white sundress, carrying a parasol. "Mister," she calls to him. "Mister."

"Mr. Licorice was mine," she says cryptically. Henry looks around to see that all the mourners are gone and just the open grave is visible in the distance.

"What?" he says to the girl. The rain is easing up as she extends her hand, beseeching him to take it. He takes her hand and she leads him toward the grave.

"Who is Mr. Licorice?" he asks her. She does not answer and continues to lead him to the open grave. As they arrive at the gravesite, the girl turns to Henry and says, "He needs help." Henry looks down into the hole in the ground and sees a black horse pawing at the wall of the grave, trying to get out.

"Please help him," the girl begs. Henry leans in for a better look. He sees that the horse in covered in blood and its eyes are bulging with distress. "Mother of Mercy, how did that animal get down—" The girl is gone and Henry is alone looking down at the helpless creature who is braying with alarm.

"Take it easy, fella," Henry says to the horse, but as he leans into the hole, his footing is on soft ground, which gives way and Henry finds himself falling into the hole. He lands on the ground below with a thud and must now avoid being trampled by an agitated stallion. Quickly he rises and looks up to the sky. The rain is still coming as a thunderclap is accompanied by a bolt of lightning.

The wall of the hole is too high for Henry to climb out. There is no one around. "Help!" he screams. "Somebody! We're down here!" he calls out.

Henry is now having the out of body experience of seeing himself in the hole with the horse, yelling for help. The horse is whinnying in distress and continuing to paw at the grave's dirt wall.

"No!" Henry calls out. "No, I can't help you," he calls down to himself. "I'm up here and I can't help you." He looks around frantically. "Somebody help!"

"Henry!" Matlida calls out to him. "Henry, wake up," she says.

Henry wakes from his nightmare with a jolt. He is in his bed with his wife, who is stroking his forehead. "It's all right, my dear," she consoles him. "You were having a bad dream."

Henry takes a moment to come back to reality. He's perspiring and clammy. He heaves a sigh and closes his eyes, then opens them and turns to Matilda, who extends her arms and hugs him. Despite her comforting gesture, an unsettling presence stays with him. He shakes his head gently, as the feeling lingers.

Delmonico's Restaurant on South William Street is renowned as the finest restaurant in America and one of New York City's most prestigious eateries. Its European-born chef, Charles Ranhofer, is a New York institution responsible for the creation of Lobster Newberg, named in honor of sea captain Ben Wenberg, and popularizing Baked Alaska, which he named to honor the recently acquired American territory. Among its well-heeled patrons are Wall Street tycoons, politicians from Tammany Hall, stars of the New York stage, real estate barons and Henry Bergh.

On an unusually mild August evening, Henry and Matilda are dining at Delmonico's with friend and newspaperman Frank Leslie and his wife, Lila. Leslie's publication, *Frank Leslie's Illustrated Weekly*, was one of Henry's most ardent supporters, and the Leslies were frequent dinner companions.

A small orchestra plays in the background as the couples are served their first course of vichyssoise, a delicate potato soup seasoned with chopped scallions and served chilled.

"So, Henry, we're all enjoying your correspondence with Mr. Barnum in the *World*," the well-read newspaperman says.

"Yes, he certainly is practiced in the field of one-upsmanship," Henry responds.

"You're not going to let him get the best of you, I hope?"

Henry takes his first sampling of the soup. "I take the moral high ground with animal abusers who wish to stage a public debate."

"I admire your tenacity. Matilda, has he always been so even-tempered?"

"My Henry has a horrible temper when it comes to animal abusers and unflattering newspaper writers."

Frank smiles. Henry is reflective. "You've been a good friend, Frank. Your paper has generated tremendous goodwill for us, and lately we need all the goodwill we can get. The *World*, the *Tribune* and the *Sun* have all been beating us up at every opportunity."

Frank offers his analysis. "After the bus company lawsuits failed, I think it galvanized your opposition. They've been spreading their smears at every opportunity."

Henry is worried. "It may be working. When we sent that laborer to jail for killing his cat, the letters we got were fierce. Some days I was afraid to open my mail."

"Three months in the penitentiary was a lot for some to swallow," Frank adds.

Henry is unwavering, "I'd have given him five for being unrepentant."

Lila chimes in at this point, "Now boys, do we have to talk business at dinner? Henry, we heard that next week is your birthday."

"Another ugly rumor," Henry snorts.

"How are you planning to celebrate?" she asks.

Matilda answers, "Bill Dunlap has invited us to one of his theatrical shows uptown. He has a fondness for dogs and horses."

"I hope you won't mind, Henry, but we've arranged a little early birthday tribute of our own."

"What?" Henry says.

Frank signals the bandleader, who ends the music and directs the musicians to play a fanfare. Waiters are seen extinguishing some of the gas lamps in the room so that the orchestra and dance floor are the only illuminated areas.

The bandleader steps forward and turns to the dinner patrons, speaking loudly enough to be heard throughout the room, "Good evening ladies and gentlemen. Tonight we have a special guest in our midst. He is the president of the Society for the Prevention of Cruelty to Animals, none other than New York's own Henry Bergh." With a sweeping wave of his arm, he points to Henry. Polite applause breaks out as Henry looks around the room with uncharacteristic embarrassment.

The bandleader continues, "To pay special tribute to his birthday next week, Delmonico's is proud to present that internationally known chanteuse, direct from her European engagement, Miss Marie Lloyd!"

The orchestra plays her on and the audience applauds as Marie Lloyd enters. She is a shapely showgirl dressed in high heels and a theatrical bustier. She crosses to the middle of the dance floor and stops, turning her attention toward the Bergh table. The orchestra begins slowly as Miss Lloyd begins to sing a slow and sultry rendition of an old nursery rhyme verse.

"Oh where, oh where has my little dog gone?
Oh where, oh where can he be?
With his ears cut short and his tail cut long.
Oh where, oh where can he be?
My little dog always waggles his tail, Whenever he wants his grog.
And if the tail were more stronger than he, Why, the tail would waggle the dog."

The audience of dinner patrons laughs and applauds sporadically, but her decidedly provocative interpretation of the song garners some sniggers from some of the male diners and raised eyebrows from some of their wives.

She slowly moves toward the Bergh table, singing as though she is seducing a man, much to the amusement of the listeners, including Henry Bergh. When she finally arrives at the Bergh table, she reaches down and swirls Henry's hair in a suggestive manner and then sits in his lap. Everyone laughs, except Henry, who merely smirks and tries to remain dignified, but there is no question he is enjoying himself. Miss Lloyd begins another chorus, flirting unblushingly with Henry as she sings.

> *"Can Mister Bergh find him in all of New York?*
> *Oh where, oh where can he be?*
> *He's searching the Bowery and Broadway, too.*
> *Oh where, oh where can he be?*
> *His men are looking from shore to shore. They wish*
> *to make their boss proud.*
> *He'll arrest the culprit that stole my poor dog. And to*
> *jail he will go with a flog."*

Laughter and applause break out as a half dozen chorus girls enter the dance floor dressed in cat costumes. The orchestra revamps to a much more upbeat, jazzy rendition of the song, as the chorus now backs up the singer with music hall style choreography. Marie gets up from Henry's lap and joins them to finish the show. The music ends with a big flourish, and the ladies receive enthusiastic applause. Henry, although still a bit embarrassed, wags his finger good-naturedly at Frank Leslie for the surprise performance. Matilda takes Henry's hand and squeezes it lovingly with the knowledge that her husband is receiving the kind of attention she can't offer him.

Henry Bergh's birthday celebration was only a temporary distraction from his growing concern about public criticism of his activities from unenlightened segments of the population or those who benefit financially from exploiting animals. He has reason to be concerned. After an unflattering cartoon in the *Sun* one day, the next morning Henry gets out of his carriage outside the ASPCA building to notice someone has thrown mud onto the bronze ASPCA plaque. The obvious act of vandalism summons up feelings of both annoyance and alarm.

Henry enters the office and matter-of-factly asks Tommy Childs to clean off the sign downstairs. He crosses to a conference table where the morning papers are placed. He picks up the papers and goes into his office. He sits at his desk, then opens the first newspaper and scans through its pages. Nothing. He takes the second paper and turns to the second page and stops with an expression of displeasure.

There is a prominent article on the page with a headline "What Is Henry Bergh?" and a subhead "Is He Notoriety Seeker or Humanitarian?"

He begins quietly reading the body copy, "Citizens are wondering if Mr. Bergh's practice of soliciting funds to carry on the work of his Society for the Prevention of Cruelty to Animals is entirely to the benefit of dumb animals, when Mr. Bergh is often seen dining at the finest restaurants, attending the opera and other theatrical amusements and leading anything but a 'charitable' lifestyle."

Henry looks up from the page with consternation. His strategy has always been to lead by example, but could the writer be right? Henry Bergh has never been filled with self-doubt with respect to his society's mission, but this is the kind of criticism that could damage his credibility and is difficult to rebut. He would have an opportunity to do just that in the afternoon at a public speaking engagement at New York University's medical college. The topic will be vivisection.

Henry arrives at University Hospital accompanied by Agents Tommy Childs and Andy Potter, who are dressed in street clothes instead of their uniforms. They enter the building and are directed to the hospital lecture hall, where Henry is greeted by Dr. Matthew

Jersey, the dean of the medical school. The white-haired doctor sports pince-nez glasses and a warm smile, which makes Henry feel welcomed. The subject of vivisection is a controversial one in the medical establishment, and Henry's hope is to sway young medical students to oppose the practice before they become engaged in it.

As doctors and students enter and take their seats in the auditorium, Dr. Jersey leads Henry to a seat on the side of the stage and then crosses to center stage to the lectern. He addresses the group, "Please come to order, gentlemen. Today's guest is the distinguished founder and president of the American Society for the Prevention of Cruelty to Animals, Mr. Henry Bergh. Please welcome him."

Polite applause greets Henry as he rises and crosses to the lectern.

"Thank you Dr. Jersey. I name this lecture, Vivisection Vivisected, because some of you gentlemen in this room, whether doctors or students, may be faced with this practice in the future, if you are not already at this time, you should be apprised of why we are opposed to such practice."

From the rear of the room a voice calls out, "Time!" which is followed by some giggles. Henry ignores the interjection.

"The presence of animals in the human community poses a number of ethical questions regarding a relationship in which there are dominant and submissive partners. Such relationship has evolved based upon our needs and values, as the dominant partners, and up to now there has been little discussion of the needs and welfare of the animals as the submissive partners."

As Henry pauses, some students in the rear momentarily cough uncontrollably, then quiet down. Henry looks up and then continues.

"Of all the horrible pangs inflicted on animal creation, those done in the name of anatomical science are at once the most fearful and revolting and the most plausibly defended. Burning, freezing, skinning alive and similar tortures in the name of science is not only a moral abomination but a useless endeavor."

Groans crop up from the audience. Henry is nonplussed.

"An animal tied down to a table and operated on with a knife is in an abnormal condition and does not answer any scientific inquiry more than the clock with its insides removed can tell the hour. Dr. Huxley once remarked that he had demonstrated that by cutting the sympathetic nerve, a rabbit can be made to blush—although Dr. Huxley cannot. The remorseless inquisitors who call themselves vivisectors are doing experiments on animals that prove nothing of value to human life."

A voice calls out from the rear of the room, "Thus spoke Zarathustra!" which is followed by some catcalls and laughter.

"I'd like to remind you that our society is also interested in the welfare of humans and human health. It was we who brought to light the scandals of diseased meat and poisonous milk. Of fish and other seafood languishing on our piers in stagnant sewer water, threatening the population with cholera and other food-induced sickness. We have worked directly with the Board of Health to reduce the sources of scourge and disease."

Faux enthusiastic applause mockingly breaks out.

"But we do not substitute one evil for another. Animals as food and animals as experiments are morally equal."

A young medical student rises and brashly calls out, "Hypocrite! Do you not eat meat?"

Henry responds without hesitation, "That is an excellent question that demonstrates that at least some of you are not hooligans with diplomas."

Some laughter validates Henry's retort.

"It's true that I can eat meat at times because of habit. If that makes me a hypocrite, then I admit my carnivorous habit as an infirmity of my humanity. But as physicians, know that the abolition of meat-eating would result in physical and moral improvement to the race. As for the casual act of devouring our animal friends, one trip to the slaughterhouse would cure most meat-eaters' desires, I assure you."

The response is met with sporadic grumbles and moans.

"I do not plead for mercy for the animals because I love them. I plead for their justice because I abhor cruelty. And you gentlemen should be practitioners of mercy, not cruelty."

Another student calls out, "We are!"

Henry looks directly at the student with incredulity, "Really?" He then reaches into his inside breast pocket and takes out a newspaper clipping and a pair of reading glasses. "Shall we talk about the cat belonging to George Bates, your late superintendent. There was a story about it in the *Mercury* last month." He puts on the glasses and looks at the news clipping. "Let's see, this reads, 'Nigger executed—the black cat at Chambers Street Hospital Hanged by Neck until Dead.' According to this reporting, Nigger was the hospital's pet cat and when Mr. Bates, his caretaker, passed on, Joe, the porter, decided he was too noisy, so he strung him up with a clothesline, while the doctors watched, quote, 'with clinical interest,' unquote. When Nigger breathed no more, his body was thrown into the ashcan."

The audience gets very quiet as Henry removes his glasses and sternly stares them down. "If this barbarous and uncivilized act was witnessed by anyone in this room, I do not hesitate to say you are unfit to be entrusted with the care of human beings. To make a farce of the dying agonies of a dumb creature is the best evidence that your profession is a cruel one, for it upholds vivisection and murders the best instincts of merciful men."

"It is wrong to equate scientists with sadists. We do not dissect animals because we desire to inflict pain," another student calls out.

"But that is the result. It is undeniable," Henry responds.

The student argues, "What is undeniable is man's quest for knowledge."

"At what expense?" Henry shoots back.

Yet another student calls out, "Let he who is free of sin cast the first stone!"

"And what is my sin?" Henry asks.

"Scandal!" a boisterous voice calls out.

The prior student responds, "We know what you do with donations to your society!"

A few students begin to chant the word "scandal." The chanting grows quickly, "scandal... scandal... scandal." Alarmed by the developments, Dr. Jersey rises from his chair on stage right and puts up his hand to the rowdy group.

"Stop it! Mr. Bergh is our guest. Stop it!" he orders.

But the crowd seems unwilling to settle down, and the usually defiant Henry Bergh views the proceedings with increasing dismay.

That night, Henry and Matilda sit down for dinner, but Henry seems uninterested in his meal.

"Henry, why aren't you eating your food?" his wife inquires.

"I'm not hungry," he listlessly responds.

"Darling, it's not like you to be discouraged. Those young doctors can't—"

"I'm not discouraged."

"What then?"

"I'm angry."

Matilda looks quizzically at her husband. He looks up and takes an envelope from his pocket and hands it to her. She takes out the letter and reads it.

Dear Henry Bergh,
Thank Heavens we found you out.
        -An Ex-Supporter

"Do you see what they're doing, Matilda? They're trying to shoot the messenger to kill the message."

Matilda takes her husband's hand. "You won't let them, Henry. That's not like you."

Illus. 31 - Puck portrays Bergh's "Dual Nature"

Illus. 32 - "I will take care of the animals," declares Bergh,
"Humanity must care for itself."

CHAPTER 13

Post-Civil War New York City is increasingly a city of contrasts. Opulent Fifth Avenue townhouses are being built to house wealthy families, such as Henry and Matilda Bergh, in growing numbers. The wealthy are prospering under Reconstruction, and a rising financial community congregating in lower Manhattan is minting newfound millionaires in every industry—the Carnegies in steel, the Mellons in banking, the Vanderbilts in shipping and railroads, the Rockefellers in oil and the Astors in real estate and furs.

At the same time, immigration into the city is rising dramatically as a result of the Irish potato famine, Russian pogroms, German and Italian homeland poverty and overpopulation and an idealized image around the world that the streets of America are "paved with gold." To the desperately poor European farmers, workers and craftsmen seeking a better life for themselves and their families, America is the destination to elevate their standard of living. They scrape together passage to the New World any way they can and travel in steamship cargo holds, passenger steerage or any other way they can get to the modern Promised Land.

Upon arriving on American shores, the reality for most immigrants quickly evaporates their fantasies of instant opportunity and wealth. Great swaths of urban landscape become large communities of tenement buildings housing immigrant families in small apartments. From Manhattan's Lower East Side to Hell's Kitchen on the west, families of all ethnicities are crowded into row after row of tenements where the day's washing hangs out the alley fire escapes to dry in the sun and the smell of ethnic cooking wafts from neighbor to neighbor. The men eke out livings as laborers, pushcart vendors or craftsmen while the women tend to the children and home. Alcoholism is rampant among many of the ethnic groups, whose men are routinely discriminated against for the best jobs and higher wages. The churches and synagogues become social centers for many families, and the public houses, or pubs, are the after-work meeting places for most working men.

The children of the poor are often expected to contribute to household expenses and put to work, sometimes as young as age five and six, in factories, textile mills, canneries and home-based businesses taking in wash or assembling various goods. Newspaper boys, also called "newsies," are the main sellers of newspapers to the general public and often not welcome with their cries of "Extra! Extra!" at all hours of the day and night. One observer of the scene writes, "There are 10,000 children living on the streets of New York. The newsboys constitute an important division of this army of homeless children. You see them everywhere. They rend the air and deafen you with their shrill cries. They surround you on the sidewalk and almost force you to buy their papers. They are ragged and dirty. Some have no coats, no shoes and no hat." Public concern for the living conditions of the newsboys is practically nonexistent.

The concept of social work to assist those in need is left largely to the religious institutions, whose legions of volunteers service the neediest as best they can. One such devotee is Etta Wheeler, a middle-aged church social worker from St. Luke's Episcopal, who attends to the elderly shut-ins and infirmed. On the first sunny day in a week, Etta is walking down West Forty-first Street where the kids are playing, pets are roaming and street vendors are hawking their goods. She stops at number 349 and enters the tenement building and walks up to the third-floor apartment of Eileen Sanders, where she knocks on the door.

"Miss Sanders, it's me, Etta Wheeler from St. Luke's."

Eileen, a frail woman in her early seventies, answers the door and invites Etta in. They proceed across the tiny, dingy apartment to the dining table. The apartment is in the rear of the building. Through the windows the buildings across the alley can be seen with laundry hanging on lines attached to the fire escapes. Eileen offers Etta a cup of tea and they sit.

"I can't go outside with ease anymore, what with my sciatica gettin' worse and the weather gettin' colder," Eileen tells Etta.

"Have you gone to church last week?"

"Not in two weeks now."

Etta consoles the old lady, "The mission will help with your groceries, Mrs. Sanders. If you make a list and give it to me, I'll be certain to go shopping for you once a week."

"Oh, Mrs. Wheeler, I can't tell you how that takes a strain off my mind. My old husband is coming home from hospital in a few days and I will need to feed him and myself. I like to cook, and standin' at the stove is somewhere I can keep warm. If you don't mind my asking, would you be—"

Suddenly, a little girl's screams are heard from outside. The girl is obviously being terrified as she wails and pleads to be left alone. Her voice is quite a distance away, but the intensity of her distress calls carries. Etta is taken back by the disturbing sounds, which eventually stop.

"By God's grace, what is happening?"

Eileen replies, "We've heard that poor child before. I don't know what apartment building she lives in, but we've all heard her screams and I pray for her every night."

Etta goes to the window as the screaming subsides and looks down the alley in search of the source. The look on her face is of both alarm and determination. She instantly decides she will find where that child is and try to help.

Leaving Mrs. Sanders, Etta walks around the corner in search of the source of the distress calls. Etta is walking by the entrance of 315 West Forty-first Street and sees a woman on the first floor hanging out at the open window. She calls up to her.

"Excuse me, can you help me? I'm looking to find someone."

The woman in window replies sharply, "Yeah, who?"

"A little girl. The neighbors hear her screams coming regular."

The woman dismisses her with a wave, as though she can't be bothered.

"Please help me find the child," Etta emplores.

"You work for the city?" the woman asks suspiciously.

"No. St. Luke's Mission. The child needs help."

The woman laughs, "You can't interfere with how a family raises their brat."

"I'm doing the Lord's work, madam. If you won't help me, some other good soul will."

The woman relents after a brief pause, "The kid's on the top floor. Back apartment. That's all I know. I minds my own business, and if you know what's good for you, you will, too. That lady has a mean temper and her husband is a bruiser. You be careful."

Etta is energized and grateful, "Thank you. I will!" She walks up the steps and enters the building.

It's a long walk up six flights, but Etta is on a mission. She quickly reaches the top floor hallway, where she looks left and right to check out the doors to the four apartments, two in front and two in the rear. She approaches the door to the rear apartment on the left and listens for any sounds as she reaches the door and waits briefly before she knocks. There is no answer.

She waits a moment longer and then turns to see the door to the apartment next door is ajar. Cautiously, she walks to that door and knocks.

From inside, a weak voice responds, "Come in."

Etta opens the unlocked door and enters an austere one-room apartment comprising a small kitchen area on one side of the room and on the other side a dresser, a chair and a bed, in which lies a very sickly old woman.

The bedridden woman looks up, "Yes, who is it?"

Etta answers her, "I'm sorry to be bothering you, ma'am. My name is Etta Wheeler. I'm a charity worker from St. Luke's Mission."

"Please, sit down," the frail, old woman replies. "I'm Mary Smitt."

Etta sits and leans into Mary so she may be heard clearly, "I'm here about your next door neighbor."

The sickly old woman looks perturbed and turns her head away as if ready to weep.

"You've heard the child, no doubt. How often does she cry out?"

Mary answers reluctantly, "For many months. Since they moved in last summer. I told Mrs. Bingham, the landlady, and she said I should mind my business."

"Have you met the woman?"

"No. She keeps to herself."

Etta continues, "And the man?"

"Not there much. I sleep a lot, due to my infirmity. When he is there, they're not a happy lot. That poor child. Can you do something to help her?"

Etta answers with determination, "I intend to, yes. May I visit you again, Mary?"

The old woman nods weakly.

Etta leaves Mrs. Smitt and walks briskly to a nearby police station. She enters the building as a patrolmen brings in a variety of ragtag criminal suspects for booking, and she proceeds directly to the desk sergeant on duty. She pleads for an officer to intervene in the abused child's case, but the sergeant shakes his head and waves her away with the excuse that child-rearing isn't under police jurisdiction. Etta won't take no for an answer. She insists that the child is being tortured and the mother needs to be arrested. That prompts him to ask her who would take care of the child in that case? An orphanage is no substitute for a parent, even if the parent is a strict disciplinarian. He remembers well the beatings he took as a boy from his father, and he's a better man for it today.

Exasperated, Etta points at him and declares that he is a barbarian and then points to the ceiling and calls on God to intervene if the police won't. She turns and exits.

Returning home, Etta is determined to get help for the unfortunate child. At the dining table, she is writing a letter to her alderman to tell the story of child abuse and the unfeeling police, when Annie, an attractive teenager, enters the room.

"My mom wants to know if you'll be home tonight."

Etta answers, "I have to go downtown. I will be back after seven o'clock."

"Is it about that girl?"

"Yes. The district attorney's office is near City Hall."

The teenager is curious, "Will he help you?"

"You mean will he help the girl?" Etta responds. "I don't know."

Etta's visit to the district attorney's office appears to be fruitful at first. She convinces an assistant district attorney to investigate the case. But he warns Etta that his office has never prosecuted the parent of a child and that juries would almost always side with a parent's authority. He agrees to take a witness statement, but short of that he can promise little. Etta leaves with some hope that her efforts will pay off.

The next day, Etta meets the attorney at Mary Smitt's building and they walk up to her apartment.

Etta and he enter and sit with Mrs. Smitt, who is in bed, and the attorney interviews her, taking notes in a pad as she speaks. He consults with Etta for follow-up questions and then returns to taking down Mrs. Smitt's observations of the neighbor's behavior and the child's predicament.

The interview lasts about fifteen minutes, and the attorney thanks Mrs. Smitt for her time and tells Etta that he will be in touch. He leaves and Etta stays with Mrs. Smitt for a short visit.

That evening, Mrs. Smitt's neighbor, Mary Connolly, a middle-aged woman with a bad disposition and a bad temper, enters her apartment from the front door and places a bag of groceries on the small kitchen counter by the stove. The tenement apartment is illuminated only by the streetlight outside. She lights a gas lamp on the wall near the stove. Then, she hears the low whimpering of a child in the next room. This angers her. She picks up a whip made of twisted rawhide tails that sits on the dining table with some cloth swatches and crosses to the bedroom.

One kerosene lamp dimly illuminates the room. A seven-year-old child dressed in rags is chained to a radiator under the windowsill, lying helplessly on the floor, weeping from the cold air that is breezing in from the partially open window.

"Stop your bawling," Mrs. Connolly demands.

The child is shivering, "I'm cold, Mother."

"You have a roof over your head! You are an ungrateful little bitch!"

As she approaches the child, fear grips the girl, "No, Mother, no."

"I told you to stop your bawling!" The angry woman bends down and grabs the child by the arm and pulls her up violently off the floor.

"Get up! How is it that I have to put up with a miserable kid like you? Look at you."

Little Mary Ellen starts crying louder.

"Shut up!" her mother screams. She lashes at the girl with the whip, hitting her on the side of the face. Mary Ellen becomes hysterical, as she is chained to the radiator and can only move a few feet away from her whip-wielding mother.

"Don't you try to run from me. This is my house! And you will pay mind to me and only me." Again Mrs. Connolly swings the whip at her little girl and strikes her arm, causing the girl to let out another shriek.

Mary Smitt is in bed listening through the common wall to the child abuse that is happening next door. The old woman is openly weeping, but too infirm to get out of bed. She reaches to the bed table where a small kerosene lamp is lit and takes hold of her Bible, clutching it to her chest. From the next room, she hears the tortured Mary Ellen pleading, "No Mama, no. Please! No! I'll be good, Mama."

"Damn right you'll be good, because you're a wicked and worthless brat. Where is your nightshirt?"

Mary Ellen answers, "I don't know, Mama."

"Well, find it, idiot!"

"Please, Mama, don't hurt me anymore."

Mary Smitt unsuccessfully tries to bury her head in her pillow as she hears more physical beating noises and the child's screams, hoping the suffering will stop sooner rather than later. The terrifying minutes that pass seem like hours.

The next day, Etta Wheeler has just climbed the stairs and heads for Mary Smitt's apartment when she sees the front floor to the Connolly apartment is ajar. Cautiously she approaches it and peeks in.

"Hello?" she says cautiously. As she slowly opens the door a bit wider she sees Mary Connolly.

"Who's there? What do you want?"

Etta answers her in her most respectful voice, "Yes, hello. I'm helping your neighbor, Mrs. Smitt, the German lady next door."

"I don't know her," Mrs. Connolly spits back.

Etta continues cautiously, "She's bedridden and very sick. She needs help."

"Well, if she's sick, keep her away from me. I can't afford to be sick what with a husband and kid to take care of," Mrs. Connolly warns.

"They sent me from St. Luke's Mission to bring groceries for the infirmed."

That seems to spark the gruff Mrs. Connolly's interest, who walks over and opens the door all the way. "Maybe next time you can bring some groceries for us. Every pay day my husband disappears and drinks our groceries for the week. I'm lucky if he brings home enough to survive."

"I'm sorry to hear that," Etta sympathizes, "You must be very strong."

Etta steps into the apartment, where in the course of the conversation, she quietly observes a barefoot little Mary Ellen washing dishes in the kitchen sink, which doubles as a bathtub, as Mrs. Connolly goes back to folding laundry at the dining table. Looking around the room Etta sees a whip with twisted leather strands sitting on the dining table and observes Mary Ellen at the sink with various marks on her arms and legs from her mother's brutal abuse. The diminutive child of seven or eight struggles with a heavy iron frying pan at the sink, her face weary with a look of suppression and misery. Etta makes a point to not let Mrs. Connolly see her observing the child and her surroundings.

"Oh yeah. I'm strong. It's the Irish in me," Mrs. Connolly answers matter-of-factly.

"Your neighbor, Mrs. Smitt, is a lovely woman. But she's very lonely and has no relatives living in New York since her husband passed."

"Poor wretch."

"Do you attend church?"

Mrs. Connolly is still folding laundry, "Not lately."

"If you are ever so moved, St. Luke's on Thirty-eighth Street has lovely services."

Mrs. Connolly doesn't look up, "I'll keep that in mind."

Etta looks around, "Well, I should be going. It was lovely meeting you. I hope you will introduce yourself to your neighbor, Mrs. Smitt, sometime. She could always use some company."

"Yeah, I'll do that," Mrs. Connolly answers blankly.

Etta, backs out of the apartment awkwardly and hesitates before she closes the door about three-quarters of the way, as she found it. She takes one last glance at the pathetic little Mary Ellen at work at the kitchen sink and with a dual look of pity and determination turns and heads for the apartment across the hall.

CHAPTER 14

Among the great outdoor spaces in New York City is Jerome Park, ninety-four acres situated in the Fordham section of the Bronx, recently annexed into the City of New York from Westchester County. The land is owned by the flamboyant Leonard Jerome, who made and lost several fortunes speculating in the stock market, earning him the title, "The King of Wall Street." He holds interests in several railroad companies in partnership with Cornelius Vanderbilt, as well as a minority interest in *The New York Times*. During the New York draft riots in July of 1863, the culmination of working-class discontent with new laws passed by Congress to draft men to fight in the ongoing Civil War, Jerome defends *The New York Times* office building with a Gatling gun against violent mobs causing destruction and mayhem. He also builds the first successful opera house in America, the Academy of Music, on East Fourteenth Street in Manhattan.

Jerome is an avid sportsman, enjoying yachting, hunting and thoroughbred horse racing. In conjunction with his brothers and the financier August Belmont, he opens Jerome Park Racetrack on September 25, 1866, marking the return of thoroughbred racing to the metropolitan area after a hiatus during the Civil War. When not residing at his stately mansion at the corner of Twenty-sixth Street and Madison Avenue, Jerome hosts events at his Bronx estate.

On a sunny Saturday morning in May, Jerome is hosting in absentia a half-dozen of his well-to-do friends to a pigeon shoot contest in the park. The gentlemen are dressed in hunting garb, carrying sport rifles and chatting among themselves while waiting for the hunt's sponsor to arrive. The pigeons are kept in wooden boxes nearby. The pigeon handler is checking his birds as two dogs sniff around near the pigeon boxes. He shoos them away.

"Have you seen any sign of Captain Bogardus?" asks Frederick Bierstadt, a Wall Street stockbroker whose brother, the well-known landscape painter Albert Bierstadt, disapproves of his sport hunting.

"Not today," answers Fernando Wood, a successful shipping merchant and former mayor of New York City.

"Then we will need to wait for him," Bierstadt instructs.

"Since the captain has the prize money, I think we have no choice," declares Joseph Jefferson III, a stage actor who became well-known for playing Rip Van Winkle.

They chuckle in agreement. In the distance, a man carrying a rifle over his shoulder can be seen walking toward the group.

"Here comes young Bennett," Wood observes, "You know he just took over his father's paper," he adds.

Jefferson responds, "He's a fine sports writer and I'm sure will make a fine editor-in-chief."

"Yes, I often read the *Herald*," says Bierstadt. "Good head on his shoulders, that boy."

James Gordon Bennett, Jr., arrives on the scene on foot, taking the rifle off his shoulder and pointing it to the ground. "Gentlemen. Beautiful day to shoot some birds, don't you think?"

They agree.

"I should warn you in advance, I intend to take home the thousand dollar prize today."

Bierstadt retorts, "Only if I go blind before the match begins."

Bennett asks, "Is the captain here?"

Wood looks off to his left and announces, "That looks like his horse over there."

From the distance, a horse and rider gallop into the scene. The horse stops and the rider, Captain Adam H. Bogardus, a corpulent man sporting an outrageously large handlebar mustache, dismounts. Bogardus is the U.S. and world champion trapshooter and is credited with popularizing trapshooting with live pigeons, which began in the U.S. around 1825. Growing up in Albany, New York, Bogardus had been shooting since he was fifteen. Before he was twenty, he had the reputation for being the best shot and hunter in his area. A carpenter by trade, he struggled to earn a living after the Civil War and soon started to hunt for a living, moving to Chicago, which had a strong market for wild game, where he could get from five to twenty-five cents a bird.

Bogardus was thirty-five years old before he took part in his first pigeon shoot, called trapshooting at the time since a live bird was released from a trap. For his first big contest, against a fellow from Detroit named Cough Stanton, he won a prize of two hundred dollars, a goodly sum in those days, after wining forty-six to forty. That match and its easy prize money made Bogardus a confirmed competitive shooter. So by 1868, he had found a new career and immediately began issuing bold challenges to other shooters. It wasn't long before he often had several matches scheduled within a week.

"Good day, gentlemen. I see we're all here," Bogardus calls out. After some small talk among the men, he loads his gun and calls to the bird handler, "Mister Sweeney, are we ready to begin?"

"Yes, sir!" says Sweeney.

"Excellent. Who's up first?" Bogardus asks.

"That would be me," Bierstadt answers.

"Then take your ready stance, mister."

Bierstadt moves into position, cocks and raises his rifle, peering down the barrel aimed at the blue sky. The bird handler has removed a bird from the box and holds it with both hands in front of him.

Bogardus pauses a moment and then shouts, "Give!"

Mr. Sweeney heaves the pigeon he is holding into the air. The bird flies as Bierstadt tries to get it in his sights. A beat later, he fires his rifle and the bird is hit, falling lifelessly to the ground. One of the dogs runs to retrieve it several hundred yards away on the ground.

"Good shot, old man," Mayor Wood congratulates him.

From the distance, a coach drawn by two horses is seen galloping feverishly toward the group. It arrives on the scene and stops, whereupon Henry Bergh and three of his uniformed agents emerge.

"Stop this event!" Bergh demands.

Captain Bogardus steps forward calmly and addresses the irate man, "Mr. Bergh, we are all aware of your opposition to this sport, but you have chosen the wrong day and the wrong group of men to impose yourself."

"Nonsense," Bergh retorts, "No man is above the law, and the court has upheld the anti-animal cruelty law with regard to this bloodthirsty endeavor."

"Not this time, old man," Bennett answers. He takes out folded papers and hands them to Bergh. "An injunction, signed by Judge Barnard, enjoining you from applying your powers to this sport within city limits."

Bergh examines the papers with surprise and exasperation.

Captain Bogardus consoles him, "Mayor Hall has great respect for your work, Henry, but he simply disagrees with you on this subject."

Mr. Bennett steps forward and addresses Bergh, "Henry, as we only live a few doors down from one another, perhaps you can overlook my participation in this as a neighborly gesture."

Bergh is not happy. "How many of the birds lie injured and suffering with broken wings or shattered beaks? And you, sir," indicating Sweeney, the handler, "do you spit chewing tobacco in their eyes to give the shooters an advantage? Or is it turpentine today? Or cayenne pepper, perhaps?"

"Mr. Bergh, please," Bogardus implores.

But Henry Bergh is relentless, "I offered you the clay disks to use in place of the birds, but you ignore a humane alternative."

"Mr. Bergh—" Bogardus tries to appease him, but Bergh will have none of it.

"Hunting is not a rational sport, but simply murder. And you are not men, but morally depraved cowards." The sportsmen look down with some embarrassment— not for themselves but for the adversary confronting them. Henry turns and waves his agents to follow him back into the carriage. "A defeat like this is only temporary," Henry thinks. "You men have not seen the last of Henry Bergh," he reassures himself.

Henry's continuing efforts would eventually have a profound effect on Bogardus's profession, as within five years the growing sentiment against the use of live birds in shooting matches resulted in laws that were finally passed in most states prohibiting the use of live birds for any kind of trapshooting, which put Bogardus and his fellow competition shooters out of work.

This new reality touched off a scramble for a substitute replacement target. One possible solution was already present in England, where a contraption called a "sling device" was in use. It threw glass balls as targets. Often the balls were filled with feathers for those who still liked to see the "feathers fly."

Charles Portlock, a Boston shooter, introduced these glass balls and traps to the United States. But the old live bird shooters didn't find them much of a challenge, as they went only a few yards in the air and a distance of thirty feet or so. Bogardus took to glass-ball shooting almost immediately. It had its drawbacks, but he had been a pioneer in the use of breechloaders and smaller shot for pigeon matches, and this new target meant he could go back to work again.

Borgadus immediately began to compete in glass-ball matches and soon developed an improved ball over the English version. One feature of them was ridges, which helped ensure that pellets would shatter the sphere, rather than glancing off, and got nicknamed "Bogardus balls." He also came up with a stronger trap, made from a wagon spring, that made Bogardus balls much harder to hit. He was now in the trap and target business.

Contemporaneously, Henry Bergh had embraced and refined the introduction and manufacture of "clay pigeons" and their mechanical launchers. The launchers were invented by a shooter from Cincinnati named George Ligowsky, who came up with the idea for a new target while watching a group of boys skipping flat stones across a lake near his home. The result was a flat clay target that would scale, spin and rise, behaving very much like a bird. These new targets made their debut at the 1880 New York State Trapshoot at Coney Island, where they soon after became the de facto standard for competition target shoots in America, "thanks to Henry Bergh's perseverance," says a proud Mary Ellen, who is now leaning forward in anticipation of what she is about to say. A slight grin comes over Allen's face, as he is amused at this elderly lady's energy, enthusiasm and stamina in telling her story.

"Yes, go on," he encourages her.

"Any time Mr. Bergh latched on to an issue, he became relentless," she says. "I was merely one of many in Mr. Bergh's portfolio. And here's how it came about."

Etta Wheeler, the St. Mark's church worker, returns home after a long day of serving the needy. The little abused child in distress continues to hang heavily in her mind. She has tried to elicit help from the police with no avail. Her local alderman was of no help either. The district attorney's office has never gotten back to her, and the child continues to suffer. She is determined to pursue the child's cause, but is running out of options. At the dinner table that evening she expresses her frustrations with her sister, brother-in-law and niece.

"It's not right that the authorities refuse to intervene on behalf of this poor child," she complains. "In a Christian society, its simply unacceptable,"

"I agree," her sister chimes in. "The mother is mentally unstable to treat the child with such violence."

"Yes, but the law does not interfere with the manner in which parents raise their children. Where would such interference eventually lead?" counters the brother-in-law.

"What do you mean?" his wife asks.

"I mean, should the state dictate where a child should be schooled or what it should wear? Where is the line drawn to override the parents?"

"The line is drawn when it is deemed torture," Etta states stoically.

"Then why don't you hire a lawyer and have the case brought to court?" he suggests.

"There's no money for that," she laments.

Annie, Etta's teenage niece, puts forth an idea that just occurs to her, "Why don't you ask for help from Mr. Henry Bergh? I read about him in the newspapers all the time. He is the man from the animal protection society. He got laws passed to protect animals from abuse."

Etta is not sure of the connection, "But, Annie, this is a child not an animal."

"If the law protects animals, should it not protect children? We are human animals are we not? The child is just a little animal."

The girl's words are inspirational. "Yes, I know of Mr. Bergh. I've read some of his writings." Etta agrees to ask Henry Bergh for help.

At the ASPCA headquarters, Henry and Elbridge Gerry are seated at the conference table with empty lunch plates and newspapers spread across the table. Henry is reading the papers to his trusted lawyer with disgust.

"'Benevolent balderdash,' writes the *World*, as he discards the paper into the trash can. 'Pigeon-hearted,' Bennett calls me in the *Herald*. And look at this, the Astor Hotel advertises its oysters are chloroformed before being opened. This mockery is outrageous. Libelous!"

Gerry tries to calm him down, "It's not libel, Henry. They're just rallying the support of the sportsmen's clubs to challenge the law. We'll quash the injunction in the Appellate Court."

"And now they're starting a fox hunting club on Long Island," Henry adds.

"Yes, I saw that in the *Sun*, but at least they quoted Oscar Wilde, 'the uneatable pursued by the unspeakable.' I rather liked that, didn't you?"

Henry shakes his head, "It's not funny."

Gerry gets up and puts on his coat. "As my mother used to say, 'Don't get your bowels in an uproar.' This fight is not over. I have to go. We'll talk tomorrow. My best to Matilda."

Gerry exits and Henry rises and crosses to his office, where he ensconces himself for the rest of the afternoon. At around four P.M., Henry is at his desk writing a letter when Agent Andy knocks on his open door.

"Mr. Bergh, there's a lady who wishes to see you."

"All right, show her in," Henry responds.

A few moments later, Andy returns with Etta Wheeler, who crosses to Henry's desk as he rises to greet her.

"How do you do, madam. I'm Henry Bergh."

Etta greets him respectfully, "Yes, I know. It's an honor, Mr. Bergh. My name is Etta Wheeler."

"Please, sit down. What can I do for you?"

Etta tells her story. "I've been everywhere. To the police. The district attorney. My alderman. No one will help me. My niece suggested I speak to you, that you might be able to do something to stop some terrible cruelty."

Henry is interested, "Yes, by all means. What sort of animal is it?"

"It's not an animal. It's a little girl. The child is an orphan. She is regularly beaten savagely by her guardian for no apparent reason. Her face and arms are cut, and she has no shoes or warm clothing. I've heard her cries and seen her condition with my own eyes."

Henry is a bit perplexed. "We are an animal protection society."

"Is a child not a little animal? Is a human being not deserving of equal treatment to a dog? The child is suffering, and no one will come to her rescue. Can't you help, Mr. Bergh? I've read your writings in the newspapers. Who will bring mercy to this helpless creature?"

Henry briefly thinks it over. "I would need proof of the situation to bring it to the authorities. Are there witnesses to the beatings?"

"The next door neighbor hears it all. Everyone in the neighborhood does, but they will not interfere," Etta explains.

Henry gives it some thought. "The case interests me, but definite testimony is necessary to warrant interference between a child and those claiming guardianship. If you would send me a written statement laying out all the facts, then I can judge the weight of the evidence at my leisure. I need time to consider if this society should interfere. I do promise to consider the case carefully."

Etta is elated, "Thank you, Mr. Bergh."

With some help from her niece and brother in-law, Etta composes the letter Mr. Bergh requested and hand delivers it to his office. Upon reading the tragic allegations relating to the abused child, Henry discusses the case with Elbridge. The two decide it has enough merit to warrant further investigation.

"The child has no one to speak for her best interests," Elbridge advises. "If she is truly being physically assaulted, she has the right to protection from the state."

Henry calls out to the next room, "Andy, come in here, would you? We have a new assignment for you."

Agent Tommy Childs is dressed in street clothes and holding a large, bound ledger book as he reaches the top floor hallway Mrs. Connolly's building. He walks down the hallway looking at the apartment numbers on the doors until he reaches the Connolly apartment. He knocks. A beat later, Mrs. Connolly comes to the door.

"Yes?" Connolly asks tersely.

Andy respectfully introduces himself, "I'm from the census, ma'am. We need some information about your household. May I come in?"

"My husband ain't home," Connolly objects.

"That's all right, ma'am. You can provide us with the information. It will take only a few minutes."

"If you must," Connolly relents. She turns with disinterest and goes back into the room. Andy follows her, checking out his surroundings carefully and observing little Mary Ellen from a distance close enough to observe her injuries.

When Andy returns to headquarters and reports his finding to his boss, that is enough to convince Henry to pursue the case of little Mary Ellen Wilson. After presenting the evidence to Elbridge Gerry, they promptly file pleadings on behalf of the child. A conference is arranged with the courts.

In the chambers of Judge Abraham Lawrence, Henry Bergh, Elbridge Gerry, Agent Andy Childs, and Etta Wheeler sit before the judge.

Gerry speaks first, "The matter is urgent, Judge Lawrence. The child in question receives regular brutal beatings and has sustained blood-letting injuries at the hands of a woman who is not the mother, but a paid guardian, receiving eight dollars a month for taking the child."

The judge turns to Henry, "Mr. Bergh, what is your interest in this case?"

Henry answers, "While we do not seek to invoke the anti-animal cruelty statute, we do believe that a child and an animal are both voiceless under the law. Does a child not deserve the same protection as a cur in the street?"

"That is a question for the Legislature. I will sign the warrant as a simple assault and battery case. Good luck," the judge advises.

That same afternoon, a posse composed of Henry Bergh, Agent Alonzo Evans and two uniformed police officers arrives at the Connolly apartment and serves Mrs. Connolly with a warrant. One of the officers then seizes the terrified Mary Ellen from the floor and holds her in his arms as she weeps and her mother demonstrably protests. The child is half naked. The second officer warns Mrs. Connolly not to interfere. He demands all the child's clothes, and Connolly indicates the rags the child is wearing is all she has. Then the four exit the apartment with the child.

CHAPTER 15

Once again, Bergh, Gerry, Agent Childs and Etta Wheeler are present before Judge Lawrence in his chambers, but this time little Mary Ellen Wilson is with them. The child holds a peppermint stick, but is still dressed in rags and showing her arm and facial wounds. A court stenographer sits to the judge's side, writing in a pad.

Judge Lawrence dictates to the stenographer, "Per the petition of Mr. Henry Bergh, this hearing is to take the testimony of Mary Ellen Wilson, a minor in the custody of the defendant, Mary McCormick Connolly. Let the record show that Miss Wilson was removed from her domicile by court order and is in the temporary custody of the state."

He turns to the child and speaks to her in an amiable tone, "Now young lady, my name is Judge Abraham Lawrence, and I want to thank you for being here today. We are going to ask you some questions, and we would like you to answer to the best you can recall. All right?"

Mary Ellen answers meekly, "Yes."

"What is your name?"

"Mary Ellen McCormick."

Gerry injects, "Let the record show that the child's birth name is Mary Ellen Wilson."

The judge continues, "Do you know how old you are?"

Mary Ellen shakes her head.

"Let the record show she does not know," the judge directs.

Lawrence turns to Gerry, who continues the questioning. "Now Mary Ellen, you live with the Connollys now, but do you remember your true parents?"

She is confused, "No. I call Mrs. Connolly 'Mama.'"

"Is what you are wearing now the only clothes you have to wear?"

"Yes."

"Have you no shoes and stockings?"

"I never had but one pair of shoes, but I can't remember when that was."

"How could you go outside in the winter if you had no shoes?"

"Mama does not let me go out of our rooms, except in the nighttime and then only in the yard."

Gerry pauses. "Who are your friends? Who do you play with?"

The girl merely shakes her head.

Gerry continues, "What do you sleep on at night?"

"A carpet under the window."

"Is it not cold under the window?"

"I have a quilt on me."

"I see. And tell us how you got the black and blue marks that I see on your face and arms and legs."

She lowers her head and answers softly, "Mama."

"How often does she beat you?"

"Every day."

"Does she beat you with only her hands?"

The girl thinks a bit, "Sometimes she uses a rawhide."

"And what about the cuts on your arm and forehead?"

"Mama used her scissors."

He shows her a large pair of scissors with an evidence tag attached.

"Are these the scissors?"

"Yes."

Gerry pauses. "Have you ever told anyone about these things Mrs. Connolly has done to you?"

"No, because I would get whipped. I don't remember ever being on the street at all. Whenever Mama went out, I was locked up in the bedroom."

"Were you ever chained to the radiator?"

"Yes."

Gerry turns to Bergh. Henry takes over, "Mary Ellen, do you remember the last time your mother, Mrs. Connolly, kissed you?"

She shakes her head.

"Does your mother ever kiss you?"

She shakes her head.

"What about holding you in her lap or touching you with a loving hand?"

She answers quietly, "No."

"Never?"

"No. She had the whip."

Henry continues probing, "When your mother whipped you, did she say why she was whipping you?"

"No. She never said why I was bad, just that I was. Most times she never said anything to me when she whipped me."

Henry asks one last question, "Do you want to go back to living with Mrs. Connolly after you leave here today?"

"No. Please, I don't want to live with Mama again." She begins crying.

Etta takes the child into her arms to comfort her. The *in camera* interview has ended. Judge Lawrence finds there is sufficient evidence to bring Mrs. Connolly to stand trial for her crimes.

A trial date is set for a mere five days later. When the day comes, it is like any other day in the New York criminal courts. Several petty crimes are on the docket for the morning session before Judge Hackett, but he disposes of the cases within an hour. At eleven A.M., Mary Ellen's case is called.

Holding a quill pen, the clerk of the court writes in a ledger book the date "April 9, 1874," at the end of a court caption, "The People vs. Mary Connolly. Felonious assault with intent to kill."

Henry Bergh and Elbridge Gerry rise from their seats and cross the room to sit with District Attorney Rollins for the prosecution. From the rear of the courtroom enters an agitated but frightened Mary Connolly with her husband, Francis, a burly man uncomfortably dressed in his only good clothes, accompanied by a court officer who directs them to be seated at the table across from the prosecutors. Judge Hackett enters the courtroom.

A bailiff calls out, "All rise. Hear ye, hear ye, this court is now in session. The Honorable Judge Hackett presiding. Be seated."

The judge reviews papers and then looks up, "Mrs. Connolly, you have been charged with the crime of felonious assault with intent to kill. How do you plead?"

Mrs. Connolly turns to her husband, who whispers in her ear. She addresses the court in a strong voice. "Not guilty."

The judge proceeds, "Very well." He turns to the prosecutor's table, "Mr. Rollins, do you wish to make an opening statement?"

Rollins stands and speaks, "Your honor, I yield to attorney Elbridge T. Gerry, representing the petitioner, Mr. Henry Bergh."

"Yes, yes, proceed, Mr. Gerry."

Gerry stands and speaks, "Thank you, your honor. Pursuant to a writ of *habeas corpus* granted by Judge Lawrence, the nine-year-old foster child of the defendant was removed from her custody upon the petition of Henry Bergh, not as president of the Society for the Prevention of Cruelty to Animals, but as a private citizen. Mr. Bergh learned of the child's barbarous treatment from Mrs. Charles C. Wheeler, who had gone to visit a dying neighbor of the defendant and was told of the frequent agonizing shrieks she heard from the child being beaten in the adjoining room. After Mrs. Wheeler inquired among the neighbors about Francis and Mary Connolly, with whom the child lived, she learned that the child was in their foster care and habitually locked in their room, had been beaten cruelly and had been left without shoes or stockings and almost without clothing during the entire winter. I submit to Your Honor the statement of the child, Mary Ellen Wilson, given to Judge Lawrence in chambers."

He hands the document to the judge, who looks it over for a moment. As he reads it, he frowns a bit in disbelief. "The court would like to see the child before it. Is she available?"

"Yes, your honor," Gerry answers.

Gerry turns and gestures to a court officer at the rear of the courtroom, who opens the door and signals to enter. ASPCA Agent Alonzo Evans, a tall man dressed in uniform holding a small figure wrapped in a gray blanket, enters the courtroom and walks down the aisle to the judge's bench. He presents the child to him by uncovering her and placing her on top of the bench. There are gasps from the gallery. The judge leans forward to view the evidence closer. What he sees is disturbing, even being a former prosecutor who has dealt with many violent crimes. The child is in such condition that the judge visibly reacts with surprise and pity. He leans back in his chair and takes a deep breath.

"Take her back and be seated," he directs Agent Evans.

Evans covers the child, carefully picks her up, crosses and sits at the end of the prosecution table next to Henry. The child turns and looks longingly at him.

"At this time," Gerry continues, "the prosecution wishes to call Mrs. Charles C. Wheeler to give testimony."

Etta Wheeler takes the stand and explains how she
first learned of the child's plight and how she felt
obliged to help, seeking help from the police, her
alderman, the district attorney and ultimately Mr.
Henry Bergh. She investigated the household by
interviewing the defendant, Mrs. Connolly, in her
apartment, where she observed the little Mary Ellen.

"I saw the child at the kitchen sink struggling with a
heavy cast iron pot. Her feet were bare. Her clothes
were ragged. She had the most despondent look on her
face, as though she was resigned to her terrible life."

Mr. Gerry asks, "And where was Mrs. Connolly?"

"At the dining table sewing. I could see on the table
a large pair of shears."

Gerry goes to the prosecution table and retrieves
large, gray scissors.

"Are these the scissors you saw, Mrs. Wheeler?"

"Yes, I believe so," she answers.

Gerry continues, "Did you observe anything else?"

"Yes, leaning on one of the dining chairs was a whip
made of twisted leather tails."

"A cat o' nine tails?"

"I suppose that's what you call it."

Attorney Gerry explains that Etta Wheeler's
testimony is the foundation for which the subsequent
investigation will reveal the criminal abuse leveled by
Mrs. Connolly against little Mary Ellen. She is excused,
and the next witness called to testify is ASPCA Agent
Alonzo Evans, who takes the oath and sits in the
witness chair.

"You accompanied the officer who brought the child
down and executed the warrant?" Mr. Gerry asks.

"I did."

"Is that the first time you had been to the Connolly's
apartment?"

"No, the day before the arrest I went there and got the name of the family and procured the name of the child."

"Did you see the child on that occasion?"

"I did."

"Did you make any inquiries of Mrs. Connolly in regard to it being her child or not?"

"I did, sir."

Mr. Gerry turns toward the defendant, "What did she say?"

"She said it was not her child."

"Did she say anything else?"

"No sir, she was very closemouthed."

Gerry continues, "How was the child dressed?"

Looking toward the child, he answers, "As she is now."

"What did the child do when you went into the room?"

"She ran into the corner of the room and crouched down in the corner and held her arms up as if she thought I was going to strike her."

"Did you make any gesture?"

"Not at all."

"What did Mrs. Connolly do?"

"She looked at me and inquired my business, and I told her."

"What happened next?"

"I left."

"When did you next see her?"

"I saw her the next morning about nine o'clock accompanied by Officer McDougal."

"Did he show the warrant?"

"He did, sir."

"What did she say when the warrant was shown to her?"

"She said, 'Do what you like with the child.'"

There are a couple of muffled gasps from female spectators in the court.

He continues, "She only wanted to know what we were taking the child for."

Mr. Gerry asks, "Did she make any other remark to you?"

"No, she was talking one thing and another. She went to the other end of the room and sat down and commenced to laugh."

"To laugh?"

"Yes sir, a kind of peculiar smile. I don't know if you could call it a smile; she did not laugh out loud."

After several more minutes of testimony describing his encounters at the Connolly apartment, Agent Evans is excused. The next witness called to the witness stand is Officer Christian McDougal, who is sworn in and identifies himself as an officer in the New York City Police Department. After reviewing some papers, Mr. Gerry puts them down on the table and turns to his witness.

"Now Officer McDougal, when you took young Mary Ellen into custody, what was she wearing?"

"Practically nothing. I wrapped my coat around her to cover her nakedness and took her to the coach."

"Did you say anything to Mrs. Connolly about the wardrobe?"

"I said to her, 'We want the clothing belonging to this child. All of it.'"

"What did she reply?"

"She produced them after a little hesitation."

"This clothing that the child wears today?"

"Yes, sir."

"Is that all?"

"I said to her, 'Is this all?' She replied, 'Yes.' 'Every Article?' 'Yes.' 'How long has she been with you?' I said. 'Six years.' 'Six years?' I replied. 'Yes, sir.' 'And that is all the clothing the child has?' 'Yes, that is all.'"

Mr. Gerry is incredulous, "No shoes or stockings?"

Agent McDougal turns to the child, "As you see her, excepting the blanket that was procured by Mr. Evans on the way down."

"What was the condition of her body in regard to bruises or marks of any kind?"

"When I got in the coach with her I retained her on my lap and covered her up with my coat and I said to her, 'What is that mark on the side of your head?' She replied that her Mama had done it. 'Did your Mama strike you?' 'Yes sir.' 'What did she strike you with?' She replied, 'The scissors.' I asked her, 'What did she strike you for?' and she replied because she didn't hold the cloth right, something that she was holding while her Mama was cutting it."

"Did she speak about any other bruises?"

"I asked her what the other bruises on the side of her head and her arms and legs were, and she said it was from a cowhide, which her mother struck her with."

The witness has an emotional moment and then composes himself to speak again. Members of the audience are visibly upset also.

"She said in general terms that her mother had whipped her repeatedly and was in the habit of whipping her."

"Did you recover the whip from the apartment?"

"I went back a second time, but I did not find it."

Mr. Gerry again pivots in the direction of the defendant, "When you returned the second time after taking the child, what was Mrs. Connolly's action, how did she deport herself?"

"She appeared excited and used language accordingly."

"Did she make any obscene remarks?"

"She made use of a very impudent remark, I thought."

"What did she say?"

"First she said I was a very pretty man or a nice looking man. Then she said, 'Would you like to come and see me?'"

Mrs. Connolly tightens her lips and looks down in shame.

"That was about it," he concludes.

The other spectators in the court glare at the defendant with disgust, making the usually plucky Mrs. Connolly visibly uncomfortable.

Officer McDougal completes his testimony, and the court recesses for lunch. Gerry and Bergh exit the courthouse, along with other court workers and observers, in search of a nearby restaurant suitable for a meal. As they cross Centre Street, they are approached by a young man carrying a notebook.

"Mr. Bergh, Mr. Gerry, my name is Jacob Riis. I write for the *Tribune*. I was an observer in the courtroom today."

Gerry and Bergh greet him. Riis establishes that he is interested in this case and intends to write about it. Always welcoming press attention, they ask him to walk with them.

"May I ask if you gentlemen intend to invoke the animal cruelty statute in this case?" Riis asks.

Gerry answers, "No, it won't be necessary. The case is about assault."

Henry adds, "Because the child is a defenseless minor, she requires an advocate on her behalf."

"And that would be you, Mr. Bergh?

"Yes."

"Why did you decide to intervene in this particular case, Mr. Bergh?"

"Common sense, Mr. Riis."

Riis presses him, "What about all the other children who suffer similar treatment? Who will advocate for them?"

Henry answers with a smile, "We're working on that, my friend. If we can protect animals, certainly the children are deserving of no less."

The men continue conversing as they walk off into the distance in search of a suitable lunch establishment.

Riis would later write about that day, "I was in the courtroom full of men with pale, stern looks. I saw a child brought in, carried in a horse blanket, at the sight of which men wept aloud. I saw it laid at the feet of the judge, who turned his face away, and in the stillness of that courtroom I heard the voice of Henry Bergh. 'The child is an animal,' he said. "If there is no justice for it as a human being, it shall at least have the rights of the cur in the street. It shall not be abused.' And as I looked I knew I was where the first chapter of the children's rights was written, under warrant of that made for the dog."

Two decades later, Jacob Riis would later go on to write a landmark book entitled, *How the Other Half Lives*, which was a terse examination of harsh tenement life in New York City. Its publication included his own photographs documenting the conditions he described. The book became widely read among the public, politicians and sociologists and came to the attention of then New York City Police Commissioner Teddy Roosevelt, who some years later, after becoming President, wrote a tribute to Riis that began: "Recently a man, well-qualified to pass judgment, alluded to Mr. Jacob A. Riis as 'the most useful citizen of New York.' Those fellow citizens of Mr. Riis who best know his work will be most apt to agree with this statement. The countless evils which lurk in the dark corners of our civic institutions, which stalk abroad in the slums, and have their permanent abode in the crowded tenement houses, have met in Mr. Riis the most formidable opponent ever encountered by them in New York City."

But on that day in 1874, Riis was only looking forward to the examination of the defendant in the afternoon session and hoping for the disposition of justice for little Mary Ellen Wilson.

Illus. 33 - Mary Ellen Wilson

CHAPTER 16

Returning to the courtroom after lunch, Mary Connolly is sworn in as a witness. She is nervous and yet cantankerous as she resentfully takes the oath and is instructed to be seated. Mr. Gerry is to question her. He rises slowly and crosses slowly to the witness chair. When he arrives he stops and turns to Mrs. Connolly, pausing with a steely eyed glare before asking his first question.

"What is your name?"

"Mrs. Mary Connolly."

"How old are you?"

"About thirty-eight years."

"Are you married or single?"

"I am a married woman at present."

"What is the name of your husband?"

"Francis Connolly."

"What is his occupation?"

"He is a butcher."

"And how long are you married?"

"About five or six years."

"Have you any children of your own?"

"I had three with my first husband: two girls and one boy."

"Where are they now?"

"They are in Heaven, I hope, where we will all be."

Gerry shoots back, "I am not so certain about that."

Connelly returns fire, "There is higher Judge who will decide."

"Yes." Gerry continues, "Where do you live?"

"I live in 315 West Forty-first Street, on the third floor."

"How many rooms do you occupy there?"

"Two."

"What are they?"

She grows indignant, "What are they?"

"Yes."

"They are dwelling rooms, of course. What do you suppose they would be?" she snorts while rearranging her skirt and scarf.

"I am examining you now, and I don't want any argument about it."

"What should two rooms be?" she sasses.

Getting back to business, Gerry changes the subject. "What is your particular occupation?"

"I do housekeeping so as to mend and make clean for my husband."

Turning in the direction of the child, "Do you know this child in court, this Mary Ellen?"

"Certainly, I should know her."

"She has been in your possession for some time, hasn't she?"

"Since the second day of January, 1866."

"Where did you get her from?"

"I got her from Mr. Kellogg."

"Who is he?"

"Don't you know the gentleman?"

Gerry turns to his witness and points at her, "I don't want any question put to me. I ask you the question. Who is he?"

Coping with his rebuke, she answers flippantly, "I don't know who he is if he ain't one of the commissioners."

"Did you know him before you went to see him about the child?"

"No," she answers matter-of-factly.

"Did you apply for this particular child?

"I did. I applied for her."

Gerry moves in a bit closer, "How did you come to apply for this particular child?"

His move makes her a bit nervous, "I wanted to keep her as my own, of course."

"Did you know anything about the child previously to applying to Mr. Kellogg?"

"Well, I did know that she was there, left as an orphan."

"From whom did you learn this?"

"I learned it from my husband—my first husband."

"And what was his name?"

"Thomas McCormick."

"Was the child any relative of Mr. McCormick?"

"I understood that she was his."

"His child?" Gerry asks.

"Yes, sir."

"Did your first husband ever tell you who the mother was?"

Connolly is uncomfortable. "No, he would not tell me. I have often wanted him to. He said she was around, but that she was good for nothing."

"Do you know who she is?"

Connolly gets steely, "No, I wish I did. I would have given her the child back long ago. Mr. Kellogg knows where she is."

"Then it was your first husband, Thomas McCormick's suggestion that you should take this child, if I understand you right?

"Yes, sir."

"And you agreed to do it?"

"I agreed to do it."

"Did you tell Mr. Kellogg why you wanted the child?"

"I told him I should like to keep it for myself. I had an idea from my husband of course telling me that there was three of his there in the asylum, two girls and a boy, and that he would like to have one out; and I said I would like to have a little girl."

"Have you ever received anything from any person for the support of this child?"

"Not one cent."

"Have you ever been promised anything by anybody for it?"

She grows indignant, "Never one cent, although they have me scandaled in the papers for it. I am thankful to the gentlemen for their scandal about me," she indicates Henry Bergh, sitting in at the prosecutors' desk. He reacts with the slightest of smirks.

Gerry continues, "Did you ever teach or cause to be taught or instruct this child in the trade of housekeeping and plain sewing?"

"When she grows up of course I will do it. I teached her the alphabet, and she can say it for you."

"Is that all you have taught her? Did you ever teach that child to pray?"

"I teached her the Lord's Prayer."

"Did you ever teach her what would become of her if she told a lie?"

Perking up, "I did often, and she is first rate for it."

"Just answer my questions. Did you ever teach her the solemnity of an oath?"

"Excuse me?"

He restates slowly, "Did you ever teach her what would become of her hereafter if she told a lie?"

"I told her she would go to the bad place if she told lies. I often teached her that."

"Did you ever teach her what you meant by the bad place?"

"Yes, that God wouldn't give her any place in Heaven."

"Did you so explain it to her?"

"I did, indeed."

"I'll ask you again, did you actually teach her the trade of housekeeping?"

"The child is too young to learn housekeeping."

"That is your idea, is it?" he presses her.

"Well, a child of eight or nine years old wants her spelling book more than she wants to do housekeeping."

"What books did you ever teach her to spell from?"

"Nothing but a plain spelling book."

"What plain spelling book?"

"Child's reading book, I have paid five and ten and fifteen cents for books for her such as that and the primer," she says proudly.

Changing the subject, Gerry asks her, "What clothing did that child have when she came with you?"

"She just had about as much as she has now."

"Nothing else?"

"Nothing else. What was on her was plain and simple, plain clothing. She had a petticoat when I got her at the place."

"She had a petticoat when she came out of the asylum, did she?"

"Yes, sir, she has a clean one now. I am not ashamed of what I wash. I am but a very humble woman myself, I can't be a lady, I can't play lady no how."

"You say when she came to you she had a flannel petticoat?"

"Yes, sir."

"What became of it?"

"I let her wear it out."

"Did you ever replace it?"

"Indeed I did. Have you been the father of a child and know what clothes you want for six years?"

"I am examining you."

Her voice grows stronger in defense, "I am the master over the child, and I keep her clean, too."

His voice grows, too, "Has the child any other clothing in your possession excepting what is now produced in court?"

Coldly, "No, she hasn't got any more clothing."

"Was the child ever sick during the time she was with you?

"She never was sickly."

"Never was?"

"She is a healthy kept child, I always kept her comfortable; she always got enough to eat and had a good warm fire, better than myself.

"When the child was removed from your custody and taken to this court, her body was covered with bruises and cuts. How can you account for that?" he demands.

Nonplussed, she answers, "I don't know."

Moving in closer again, "Did you inflict such wounds on Mary Ellen Wilson, your legal ward?"

"No."

"Then how did such marks and cuts find their way to the poor child's body?"

"They must be from playing in the alley."

Gerry goes to the prosecution table and retrieves a pair of scissors. "These scissors were taken from your house, Mrs. Connolly. Do you recognize them?"

Reluctantly, she answers, "Yes."

"Have you ever used these scissors against young Mary Ellen?"

At this point the judge intervenes, "Mrs. Connolly, I must advise you that you have a right against self-incrimination. You may invoke such right at this time if you wish to refuse to answer this question."

Mrs. Connolly merely hangs her head down in silence.

Mr. Gerry has made his point. "No more questions."

Little Mary Ellen is sitting comfortably in the courtroom on the lap of Henry Bergh. The pathetic little girl is keenly aware that she is finally rescued from her hellish life at the Connollys. Her face shows it.

It is the same face that seven decades later sits in her sunroom in Upstate New York seated comfortably in her favorite easy chair, talking to a television news crew. She concludes her tale.

"Mrs. Connolly was convicted and was punished with a year in jail. I never saw her again," she states calmly.

Allen, her interviewer, asks, "And Mr. Bergh?"

"Mr. Bergh went on to found the first Society for the Prevention of Cruelty to Children, which was the beginning of the reforms in child labor laws and all that. I never saw him again, either. He died the year I got married, in the blizzard of '88."

The story Mary Ellen tells is seen and heard by millions of television viewers just a short time after it was recorded on film. Whether in person or on a black and white television, the life she describes is filled with the same drama and compassion that keeps listeners riveted to her tale.

"I owe my life to Henry Bergh. Without him, I probably would not be here today. His message of mercy and compassion for all living things and his utter commitment to changing the way we think and the way we act as a civilized society has made the world a better place, and that is why we all owe Henry Bergh a debt of gratitude."

The television set with Mary Ellen's face on it is in the window of a television store with the same picture displaying on all the TV sets. It is night and the flickering images on the screens catch the eyes of some pedestrians who pass by and watch for a brief moment. The end credit logo of *CBS Reports* appears on the screen as the TV announcer speaks.

"This has been *CBS Reports* with Douglas Edwards. Stay tuned for your local news. This is the CBS Television Network."

From the loudspeaker mounted on the outside of the store window, the program music crests and subsides as the pictures on the TVs fade out and then fade up into a Speedy Alka-Seltzer commercial. A man walking his dog passes by the store as the city traffic rumbles on the avenue and evening pedestrians go on their ways.

EPILOGUE

In the twenty-two years Henry Bergh was president of the ASPCA, thirteen thousand cases of cruelty to animals were prosecuted, and similar animal protection societies were formed in thirty-nine states as well as in six Canadian cities.

Today, there are more than one hundred fifty national animal protection organizations and thousands of local groups.

Bergh's efforts on behalf of children led to the establishment of the first Society for the Prevention of Cruelty to Children and the reform of the child labor laws as we know them today.

Even P.T. Barnum, with whom Bergh fought in public, had enough respect and affection for him and his crusade to leave $1,000 in his will for the erection of a statue in Bridgeport, Connecticut, honoring Bergh.

Henry and Matilda Bergh's final resting place is in a pyramid-shaped monument at the Green-Wood Cemetery in Brooklyn, New York.

The noted American poet Henry Wadsworth Longfellow wrote this tribute to the man dubbed "The Great Meddler":

Among the noblest of the land,
Though he may count himself the least,
That man I honor and revere,
Who without favor and without fear,
In the great city dares to stand,
The friend of every friendless beast.

It is ironic that despite starting the first animal protection organization in America, Henry Bergh never had any pets, and despite starting the children's protection movement, he never had any children. Henry

Bergh is a pivotal historical character in the story of this nation. He was responsible for the birth of two great social justice movements, and yet he remains relatively unsung and unknown. No doubt, he is the most famous American you've never heard of.

Illus. 34 - Henry Bergh (1813-1888)

AUTHOR'S NOTES

Principal sources for this novel include the personal journals of Henry Bergh, as well as newspaper and magazine clippings, court transcripts and summonses, as preserved in the archives of the ASPCA in New York City and the New York Public Library. Also referenced is *Angel in Top Hat* by Zulma Steele (1942, Harper & Brothers); *Henry Bergh, Founder of the A.S.P.C.A.* by Alvin F. Harlow (1957, Julian Messner, Inc.); *New York by Gas-Light* by George G. Foster (1850); *A Renegade History of the United States* by Thaddeus Russell (2010, Free Press/Simon & Schuster, Inc.); *The Mary Ellen Wilson Child Abuse Case and the Beginning of Children's Rights in 19th Century America* by Eric A. Shelman and Stephen Lazoritz, M.D. (2005, McFarland & Company, Inc.); *The Quality of Mercy: Organized Animal Protection in the United States 1866-1930* by Bernard Oreste Unti (2002, American University doctoral thesis); *The Fabulous Showman, The Life and Times of P.T. Barnum* by Irving Wallace (1959, Alfred A. Knopf, Inc.); *The Gangs of New York* by Herbert Asbury (1928, Alfred A. Knopf, Inc.); *The Great Meddler,* story by Joseph Ansen, screenplay by Barney Gerard and Julian Hochfelder (1940, MGM); *The Great Adventure: The Great Crusader,* story by Clyde Ware, teleplay by Margaret Shea and John Mantley (1964, CBS); as well as numerous Wikipedia entries and other published articles. Lyrics to *The Glow* Worm were originally written by Paul Lincke and adapted by Johnny Mercer (© 1952 by Carlin America Inc.).

As a novel, I have tried to tell the story of Henry Bergh and his achievements as a story and not as a history. The accounts of his life as documented in his journals and the contemporary press are portrayed accurately, and many of the words spoken are faithful to such records. Other characters, scenes and dialogue have been dramatized to reflect aspects of a three-dimensional, flesh and blood human being whose motivations and private thoughts may never have been recorded, but undoubtedly resulted in his actions.

Chapter 7 has been adapted from George G. Foster's 1850 book, *New York by Gas-Light* and does not necessarily reflect Henry Bergh's personal story. It and other intimate encounters and thoughts attributed to Henry Bergh were reasonably included to speculate that all men share certain private feelings and experiences that contribute to their psychological makeup, and it was presented to possibly explain the origins of Henry Bergh's strong personality and the motivations for his activism, after drawing inferences from his writings, particularly his poems and plays.

The portrayal of Mary Ellen Wilson as an adult, whose married name was Mrs. Schutt, has been dramatized, and the characters of the television news crew are fictional.

Lastly, I wish to thank Valerie Angeli at the ASPCA for generous access to its archives, which contains a treasure-trove of Henry Bergh materials, and brought the author only one degree of separation from the founder of the modern animal and children's protection movements in this country. Not coming from the academic community, this author was truly inspired to touch the very documents upon whose hand Henry Bergh himself wrote his words. The author hopes this book will inspire its readers to take up the causes Mr. Bergh began so many years ago, or at the least make the consumer choices that support its spirit.

ILLUSTRATIONS

Illus. 1 - drawing of young Henry Bergh, date and artist unknown

Illus. 2 - photograph of young Henry Bergh, date and photographer unknown

Illus. 3 - painting of Richard Martin, courtesy of the RSPCA

Illus. 4 - illustration of the trial of Bill Burns, 1838, courtesy of the RSPCA

Illus. 5 - William Hogarth etching, "First Stage of Cruelty," 1751

Illus. 6 - William Hogarth etching, "Second Stage of Cruelty," 1751

Illus. 7 - William Hogarth etching, "Cruelty in Perfection," 1751

Illus. 8 - William Hogarth etching, "The Reward of Cruelty," 1751

Illus. 9 - photograph of Henry Bergh, c. 1860, courtesy of his grand-niece, Mrs. Walter Jennings; photograph of Elbridge T. Gerry, courtesy of the George Sim Johnston Archives of The New York Society for the Prevention of Cruelty to Children

Illus. 10 - "City Enormities—Every Brute Can Beat His Beast," 1865, *Frank Leslie's Illustrated Weekly*

Illus. 11 - 1876 woodcut of ASPCA headquarters at Fourth Avenue and Twenty-second Street, artist unknown

Illus. 12 - ASPCA emblem, c. 1886

Illus. 13 - "Arrested for Cruelty", by C.S. Heinlet, from *Harper's Weekly*, January 13, 1872, courtesy of The New York Public Library

Illus. 14 - "Mr. Bergh to the Rescue," Thomas Nast
        cartoon

Illus. 15 - "The Friend of the Brutes," by J.A. Wales,
        courtesy of The New York Public Library

Illus. 16 - 19th century woodcut of dogs being drowned in
        East River, artist unknown

Illus. 17 - Dog fighting at Sportsmen's Hall, date and
        artist unknown

Illus. 18 - Rat baiting at Sportsmen's Hall, date and
        artist unknown

Illus. 19 - The Arrest of Kit Burns, signed Bghs

Illus. 20 - Henry Bergh's horse derrick, date and artist
        unknown

Illus. 21 - ASPCA animal ambulance, date and artist
        unknown

Illus. 22 - 19th century photograph of Pullman Company
        boxcar

Illus. 23 - Cattle being transported by boxcar to
        slaughter, date and artist unknown

Illus. 24 - "The Crowded Car," by Sol Etyinge, Jr., from
        Harper's Weekly

Illus. 25 - Overloaded streetcar, date and artist
        unknown

Illus. 26 - photograph portrait of Phineas Taylor (P.T.)
        Barnum

Illus. 27 - "View of the American Museum, Broadway,
        New York" by Chapin, 1886

Illus. 28 - "The Only Mourner" by A Wales, from *Puck*

Illus. 29 - "The arrest (afterwards imprisonment), for
        killing a cat, although provoked to the act by a
        cat-nip. (*Respectfully* DED-I-CAT-ED *to the
        man of* FELLEN (e) Mr. H. Reeburg, *President
        of the Society for the Invention of Foolery about
        Animals*.)," drawn by J.C.Mon., 1878

Illus. 30 - "Mr. Bergh's Steam Flogging Machine" drawn by Joseph Keppler, from *Puck*, courtesy of The New York Public Library

Illus. 31 - "Mr. Bergh's Dual Nature" from *Puck*, courtesy of The New York Public Library

Illus. 32 - "I will take care of the animals; humanity must care for itself," courtesy of The New York Public Library

Illus. 33 - photograph of Mary Ellen Wilson courtesy of the George Sim Johnston Archives of The New York Society for the Prevention of Cruelty to Children

Illus. 34 - Henry Bergh etching from newspaper obituary, c. March 12, 1888

CPSIA information can be obtained at www.ICGtesting.com
Printed in the USA
LVOW13s0348231013

358115LV00001B/2/P